"You married me, not for myself, but for the price of a ring!"

"The Ravenelli Ruby is priceless...."

"Priceless? Is anything of more value than a human heart?" Amy cried.

"I gave you what you wanted. I married you. You had my ring on your finger, my name. You had my wealth. You still have all those. What more could you want?"

His love. All that Amy had ever wanted was Vincenzo's love, and without that, nothing had any value.

"What if I don't want this marriage to continue?" Amy asked.

"I told you, *carissima*, that is not an option."

"But surely you would prefer to be free—to marry again?"

"*You* are my wife." It was harsh, inflexible, totally unyielding.

VIVA LA VIDA DE AMOR!

They speak the language of passion.

In Harlequin Presents®, you'll find a
special kind of lover—full of Latin charm.
Whether he's relaxing in denims or dressed
for dinner, giving you diamonds or
simply sweet dreams, he's got spirit,
style and sex appeal!

Latin Lovers is the new miniseries
from Harlequin Presents®—
for anyone who enjoys hot romance!

Look out for our next **Latin Lovers** title:
Duarte's Child
by
Lynne Graham
Harlequin Presents #2199
Available in September

Kate Walker

HER SECRET BRIDEGROOM

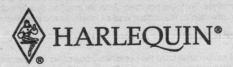

HARLEQUIN®

TORONTO • NEW YORK • LONDON
AMSTERDAM • PARIS • SYDNEY • HAMBURG
STOCKHOLM • ATHENS • TOKYO • MILAN • MADRID
PRAGUE • WARSAW • BUDAPEST • AUCKLAND

ISBN 0-373-12191-1

HER SECRET BRIDEGROOM

First North American Publication 2001.

Copyright © 2000 by Kate Walker.

Visit us at www.eHarlequin.com

Printed in U.S.A.

CHAPTER ONE

'THERE has to be some mistake!'

Amy stared up at the imposing building before her, her nerves, already tightly knotted, taking on an extra twist of tension as she took in its size and elegance.

'This can't be right!'

Her answer was a stream of incomprehensible Italian, the water taxi driver nodding his head emphatically, his tone indignant. The only words she picked out were 'Ravenelli' and *'palazzo'*, which seemed to confirm that he had indeed taken her to the destination she had requested.

But not to the place she had anticipated. When she had last been in Venice, the home of the particular Ravenelli male she was looking for, the home she had shared with him for so brief a time, had been a far less awesome structure.

'But...*signore*,' she managed hesitantly, 'I...'

The driver's response was another string of fast, indignant eloquence, accompanied by much hand-waving and animated gesturing.

'Please!' she tried again. 'I wanted the home of Signor *Vincenzo* Ravenelli. He—'

'And you have found it,' another voice broke in. A deep, delightfully accented voice that still, much to Amy's annoyance, had the power to send shivers of sensual reaction running down her spine. 'You have found my home, and at last you have found me, my sweet wife.'

Too late, Amy realised that the driver's second outburst had been directed out of the window and not towards her. And his wildly waving gestures had been designed to draw her attention to the man who, attracted by the altercation

5

outside, had come to the door to find out what was going on.

Panic struck hard and sharp. For the space of perhaps a dozen frantic, uneven heartbeats, she was severely tempted to tell the driver to turn, to put his foot down and move away—*fast*, but almost immediately she reconsidered.

To show her fear, to show any sort of reaction at all, would be playing straight into Vincenzo's hands. If she bolted like a panic-stricken deer at just the sound of his voice, then she would never again be able claim that he no longer meant anything to her.

And so she forced her hypersensitive nerves back under ruthless control, stilled the frantic breathing that betrayed her with the way her breasts rose and fell under the tailored grey linen of her dress, and managed to turn to face him, switching on a smile that was blatantly false and insincere.

'Hello, Vincenzo.'

It was all she could manage so she had to be grateful for the fact that she sounded cool and distant, the impression she was aiming for, and not as she actually *felt*. That was a far more complicated matter, made up of opposite conflicting emotions, some of which her mind and heart rejected violently while other, less rational senses responded in a flurry of primitive excitement.

'You haven't changed.'

Understatement of the year. If only he *had* changed. Or if the distance of the years since she had last seen him had added some perspective to her view of him so that she was able to regard him calmly and with a degree of objectivity lent by the passage of time.

But would any amount of time blunt the impact of a lithe, muscular physique, a powerful chest, narrow waist, and long, long legs? What force could leave her immune to jet-black hair that gleamed like polished onyx in the afternoon sun, equally coal-dark eyes set above sharply carved cheekbones, and fringed with the sort of thickly luxuriant lashes that somehow only intensified rather than softened their fierce brilliance?

No woman she knew could focus her eyes on the smooth olive skin, the stunning features, just once and not come back, greedily, for a second look. And in spite of everything she knew about him, in spite of the pain, the humiliation he had doled out to her with careless cruelty, neither could she.

'Y-you're looking well,' she managed inanely. What little composure she had left had been wrenched from her by the realisation that he had come right out of the house and was standing, tall and proud, beside the boat so that she had to tilt her head up at an awkward angle to see him.

'I wish I could say the same for you,' was the sardonically drawled response. 'But I'm afraid that you have me at a disadvantage, lurking in there like some small rodent in its hole. So tell me, *moglie mia*, do you intend to get out of the boat, or are you planning on staying there all afternoon?'

'If you'll just let me p-pay the driver...' Amy spluttered indignantly, grabbing for her handbag and hunting through it.

'Allow me.'

Before she even had time to open her purse, Vincenzo had pulled out the requisite money and in an imperious gesture proffered it to the driver, whose eyes lit up at the sight of what was obviously an inordinately extravagant tip.

'Thank you.'

It came through gritted teeth. Only the belated realisation that the driver had been a silently fascinated audience to their earlier exchanges, his eyes practically out on stalks at the sound of that casual claiming of her as *'moglie mia'*— my wife—*forced* Amy into accepting Vincenzo's autocratic interference and swallowing down her instinctive protests.

Time enough for those later, she told herself, determined not to be dragged into an embarrassing scene out here in public. She could pay back Vincenzo, both financially and emotionally, once they were inside and away from prying eyes.

The driver's reaction had reminded her that, even in the sophisticated and cosmopolitan society of Venice, the Ravenelli name was famous, and not just for the production of exquisite and outrageously expensive glass which had formed the backbone of the family fortune for more than three centuries. No doubt the actions of the eldest son of that rich and powerful family would provide plenty of scope for the gossip columns of the more popular newspapers, and she would do well to try and avoid any further attention.

Vincenzo, however obviously had no such compunction.

'Anything for you, *carissima*,' he returned, deliberately laying it on thick. He didn't quite produce a courtly bow as he bent to offer her his hand to help her out of the bobbing boat, but his actions had something of the same elegant courtesy that successfully hid the way he must be feeling, she thought on a shiver of reaction.

'My bag...' Amy managed as she struggled to clamber out with a matching elegance, all the while ignoring the hand he held out to her in spite of the awkwardness of manoeuvring. To touch him, feel those strong, bronzed fingers close around her own, as they had done so often in the past, would be more than she could bear.

'Guido will see to it.'

Another of those lordly gestures indicated the short, stocky man who, summoned by some silent sign Amy had been unable to catch, had emerged from the house and was already taking her suitcase from the driver.

'Is that all?' Vincenzo questioned, frowning at the sight of the small, slightly battered canvas case.

'All I wanted to bring with me!'

She hadn't been planning on a long stay. But it was more than that. Amy felt absurdly indignant on behalf of her luggage. The scathing look Vincenzo had turned in its direction seemed to hold all the contempt and scorn he had once displayed for her feelings.

'After all, I left almost all of my clothes behind.'

'So you did. But what makes you think that I kept them? Did you not assure me that you were out of my life for good; that you never planned on coming back—ever?'

'Circumstances change!'

'So they do.'

His smile in response to her tartness was a mere flicker, there and then gone again in a second. It left no impression of warmth, but rather the opposite, a sensation like the cold slither of something slimy worming its way down Amy's spine.

'However, *cara*, I seem to recall that when I predicted that this might happen, your only response was to shut your door firmly in my face. But perhaps we should continue this conversation inside. You must be tired after your journey, and would like to freshen up.'

'A drink would be welcome.' Amy matched his cool politeness tone for tone. 'And I'd be glad to get out of the sun.'

And perhaps after a short time to recover, to ease the unnatural dryness in her throat, restore some degree of balance to thoughts badly shaken by Vincenzo's unexpected appearance, she might find the nerve to explain to him exactly why she had come. But not now. Not when her courage seemed to have deserted her completely, driven away by the sort of response that was the exact opposite of the one she had anticipated.

When she had considered how Vincenzo Ravenelli might react to her unexpected appearance back in his life, she had not expected this sanguine indifference. If the truth was told, she had imagined him behaving in much the same way as she had responded to him almost four years before, when he had followed her to England and insisted on seeing her.

Terrified by the ease with which he had tracked her down, and in agony over the cruel betrayal he had just subjected her to, she had been unable to control the whirling panic in her brain and had resorted to the only form of action she could think of. The slam of the door to her mother's house, literally right in that sneering aristocratic face, still reverberated through her dreams, plagued by unwanted memories.

'Then come indoors.'

With another of those courtly gestures, he stood back to let her precede him over the threshold.

'Welcome to my home.'

Will you walk into my parlour? said the spider to the fly... Unwanted, the words to the old rhyme resounded inside her head, making her steps unsteady and hesitant. Just what did Vincenzo have in mind, once he had her in his domain? Suddenly she regretted leaving even the dubious protection of the fascinated taxi driver.

Two steps inside the house Amy froze, staring in transfixed amazement at the sheer size and splendour of her surroundings, the breath leaving her lungs in a gasp of shock and admiration.

Below her feet a polished marble floor glowed like soft coral. The high cream walls were bare except for a huge, ornate, gold-framed mirror that stood above an equally ornamental gold-painted table, framed in their turn by the enormous windows with heavy, dark wooden shutters. Shafts of sunlight slanted through the glass, pooling softly on the floor, and beyond the window the waters of one of Venice's famous canals lapped slowly and lazily in the afternoon warmth.

'It's beautiful!' The words sprang from her lips in spontaneous delight. 'And so big! I almost feel as if I'm in a—a cathedral instead of a house. But when did you come to live here?'

When she had known him before he had had an apartment in another part of the city. A large, elegant, luxurious apartment, true, but nothing to compare to this splendour.

'This is the family home.'

Something in Vincenzo's voice tightened on her nerves, twisting the knots of tension up several degrees so that she swung round sharply, catching the shadow of something in his aristocratic face before he could mask it carefully.

'My father died last year.' It was cold and clipped and utterly rejecting of any expression of sympathy before it even had time to form. 'I inherited the house in his will. The house and the vineyards, and the whole of the Ravenelli business empire.'

Amy's eyes widened, their already deep blue darkening to almost navy in shock.

'All of it?'

He had been wealthy in his own right before, but if he now owned and ran his father's businesses as well, then his wealth was probably in the multi-millionaire class.

'All of it,' Vincenzo assured her with another of those swift, dismissive movements of his head. 'So you see, *mia cara*, you are now the wife of a very wealthy man indeed.'

In spite of her determination to hang onto her control, his careless words pressed buttons that were dangerously close to the surface.

'I was never really your wife, not in any true sense of the word!' It was impossible to hide the way that made her feel. 'Our marriage, such as it was, was a lie from start to finish. Tell me, Vincenzo, is that how you usually work?'

'*Amy!*'

Her name was a sound of warning. A warning the twist of anguish deep inside drove her to ignore.

'Do you usually have to entice women into your bed with deceit and lies? Isn't it possible—'

'*Per Dio*, Amy, enough!'

He hadn't raised his voice, but the words slashed at her in a tone of such suppressed violence that they killed the rest of her comments in her throat, leaving her floundering. Seeing the dark cast of anger on his handsome features, the cold blaze of it in his eyes, she was fearfully aware of the risks she had taken in overstepping the mark so far, so fast.

Careful! she warned herself reprovingly. You want his co-operation, not his hostility. It wouldn't do to be so antagonistic from the first that Vincenzo would refuse to have anything to do with what she had come here to ask. But the memories had hurt so much that it had been impossible to hold back.

'I…' she began, but Vincenzo had already directed his attention elsewhere.

'Guido.'

Whirling round, Amy belatedly became aware of the manservant's hovering presence at the base of a wide, curving flight of marble stairs and her insides clenched nervously at the realisation that Vincenzo had been so blackly furious because her unthinking words had been flung at him in the other man's presence.

'Take the *signora's* case upstairs. The blue room.'

'Oh, but…' This was not what she had planned at all. 'I won't be staying here.'

A look of such fierce scorn raked over her that she was surprised she was still standing and hadn't been shrivelled to ashes where she stood.

'And where else would you stay?' he enquired in a tone so cold it seemed to freeze the blood in her veins.

'Well, I—I would have thought—in an hotel.'

An imperious gesture with one long-fingered hand dismissed her stumbling suggestion with arrogant contempt.

'*Impossibile*. You are my wife, and as such, naturally you will stay here. Guido…'

But the manservant was already on his way up the stairs. Clearly he had too much respect for his employer's volatile temper to risk having it turned on his unfortunate head if he seemed to question or hesitate to obey the autocratic command.

Seconds later Amy was to wish she had taken the same prudent course as Vincenzo rounded on her, black eyes blazing, ruthlessly reined-in anger etching white marks around his nose and mouth. She had no time to protest, instead finding her wrist caught in a punishing grip as she was bundled unceremoniously out of the hall and through one of the high doorways into an elegant sitting room beyond.

Kicking the door to behind him, Vincenzo came to a halt in the middle of the room and turned to face her, holding her captive hand up between their two bodies as his breath hissed savagely between his teeth.

'I realise, *bella mia*, that we have a great deal to talk about, that there is a lot of unfinished business between the two of us—but I will thank you to keep such matters where they belong—in private. I do not want the world knowing the messy details of my marriage, and the reasons why you have not lived with me for the past four years.'

'N-neither do I,' Amy admitted shakily.

After all, wasn't that why, ever since the moment she had fled from Venice four years before, she had never admitted to anyone that she actually *was* married? Even her own mother was blissfully unaware of the appalling consequences of the apparently innocent Italian holiday she had given her daughter as a present for her twentieth birthday.

Like everyone back in England, Sarah Redman knew nothing of the foolish naivety, the blind, deluded emotion that had rushed Amy into the marriage that she had come to see as the worst and most bitterly regretted mistake she had ever made in all of her twenty-four years.

'So we are agreed, then? In public you are my wife and you will keep a civil tongue in your head.'

She'd really stung his fierce male pride, the pride that

made it impossible for Vincenzo Ravenelli to be seen as anything other than the brightest and the best. The most successful; the most powerful. The man who had the world at his feet, whose life was perfection in everything.

Except in his marriage.

Now was the time to tell him the truth. To tell him exactly why she was here, in Venice, in his house. To let him know that she wanted their farce of a marriage to end; that she wanted a divorce.

But even as she opened her mouth to frame the words she looked into the darkness of his eyes, saw the barely suppressed fury still smouldering there, and her courage deserted her in a rush.

'And—in private?' was all she managed to croak.

'In private?' Vincenzo echoed, his voice dropping an octave, taking on a disturbingly husky note.

His dark eyes were suddenly caressing as they moved slowly and intently over her face, lingering on her wide, almond-shaped eyes, the soft fullness of her lips. What she saw in their darkness made her swallow hard, but with a very different reaction to the tension of a moment before.

'In private, *cara mia*, we will see. I have waited four long years for you to see sense and return to me, I reckon I can wait a little while longer.'

Long brown fingers trailed a soft path down the side of her cheek and the pad of his thumb smoothed over the fullness of her mouth with a delicate sensuality that had her lips parting on a faint gasp of shock.

'You see...'

Vincenzo's sensuously triumphant smile told her that, infuriatingly, he had interpreted her reaction as one of pleasurable response to his caress and not the indignation she had really felt.

'Already it begins, *moglie mia*. Already we have moved from the cold distance of miles to something better. Something that tells me you will soon forget the foolish pride that has kept you away from me for so long, and remember how it used to be.'

He really believed what he was saying, Amy told herself, her head spinning at the thought. He was truly convinced that all he had had to do was to wait, to sit here in all his lordly arrogance, and eventually she would come crawling back to him. That she would kneel at his feet begging him to forgive her for walking out on him, and pleading to be taken back!

Well, he had another think coming! She would rather die than let him delude himself any longer! It was time he learned the real reason for her being in Venice. Temper or not, she was going to tell him right now!

But even as she opened her mouth to fling the truth straight into his smiling face, Vincenzo bent his dark head and took her lips in a kiss so soft, so gentle that it seemed to reach down deep inside her and draw out her soul from the very depths of her being. And when he took his mouth away again all she could manage was a long drawn-out sigh that might equally have been a sound of delight or of rejection, even she could not say.

'You do remember, don't you?' Vincenzo's breath was warm against her cheek, his voice a tiger's purr, as rich with confidence as his smile. 'How it once was. How it can be again.'

'How it was?' Amy repeated tartly jerking her head away from his imprisoning fingers, blue eyes flashing defiance into the onyx gleam of his. 'You mean the mindless physical attraction I had for you that conned me into believing I felt something more? I was itching for an affair, and you came along at the right moment, that's all. If you thought it was anything more than my hormones going into overdrive, then I'm afraid you're very much mistaken!'

If she had expected to shake him, she was desperately disappointed. If anything, he looked even more confident, that arrogant smile growing wider until she had to clench her fingers hard against the temptation to lash out and wipe it from his handsome face.

'So, the kitten has claws after all,' he drawled softly. 'And that is just the way I would have wanted it. I wouldn't have wanted you to fall straight into my fingers like a ripe plum—where is the pleasure in that?'

'Wha—what do you mean?'

'In matters of the heart, *innamorata*, the chase can be every bit as exciting as the actual moment of possession. The delay only whets the appetite, strengthens the desire. So fight me all you can, *bella mia*, but you're only fighting the inevitable. You will have to give in sometime, and your surrender will be all the sweeter for the waiting.'

'Never!' Amy managed to gasp, her blood curdling at the sound of his laughter.

'Never is a delusion, my sweet Amy. You know it and so do I. We were made to be together. The one hot night we shared—our wedding night—was enough to tell me that.'

But that one night was all he was ever going to know, Amy resolved in the privacy of her own thoughts. Their marriage had ended less than twenty-four hours later, and she was determined to finish it now—once and for all.

But first she would have a little private satisfaction. She would take this arrogant, self-confident pig and play him at his own game for a while.

Then, and only then, would she tell him the truth.

She reckoned it would go some way towards avenging the anguish that he had put her through four years ago.

CHAPTER TWO

'YOU offered me a drink...'

Amy eased herself from Vincenzo's restraining arms with as much coolness as she could muster and moved away, deliberately putting a distance that was as much emotional as physical between them.

'I really am very thirsty,' she said, automatically smoothing down the dark silk of her hair where his strong fingers had tousled it. 'And tired...'

His smile told her that he knew exactly what she was doing but, to her relief, he simply nodded.

'What would you like? Tea? Mineral water? I'll have it brought to your room, shall I?'

'*My* room?' Amy questioned sharply and met another of those fiendishly knowing glances.

'Of course I have provided you with a separate room, *cara mia*. Credit me with a little finesse. We both know why you are here, but that does not mean I am not prepared to allow you a little time to adjust. We have been apart many times longer than we ever were together. We need to get to know each other again.'

She knew everything she ever wanted to know about him! What else could she possibly learn other than that his smooth, sophisticated exterior hid an even more cruel and hateful personality than she had ever expected? She had been so bitterly deceived by that veneer of courtesy and gentleness—but never again!

'Yes, I would like some time in my room,' she managed, praying that Vincenzo's sharp, assessing eyes wouldn't catch the difference in her mood, the change in her expression. 'I'd like to freshen up—take a rest.'

'But of course.'

Immediately Vincenzo was all courtesy, the mask of civility quickly back in place.

The room he took her to was magnificent. Decorated in the softest tones of blue, occasionally highlighted with a rich cream, it had a high ceiling and beautifully colour-washed walls. A huge bed, piled high with downy pillows and draped in silk, seemed to whisper sensual promises of soft comfort and deep, relaxing sleep.

To her left, a door stood half-open, revealing a beautifully equipped en suite bathroom. And on the far side, opposite to the door, large, arching windows, draped like the bed, let in the warmth of the Italian spring sunlight that was so very different from the grey clouds and damp days she had left behind in the north of England.

'It's beautiful!' Amy managed because she felt obliged to say something.

'Your enthusiasm is overwhelming.' Vincenzo had caught the flat note in her voice that she hadn't been able to disguise.

'Well, you know me...' Amy blustered awkwardly, immediately wishing she hadn't used precisely those words.

The smile curling Vincenzo's beautifully shaped mouth, a disturbing light in his eyes made her heart lurch uncomfortably, setting up a heavy, uneven rhythm that brought a rush of unwanted colour to her cheeks.

'I find all this magnificence a bit impersonal—a showplace, not a home. I prefer something simpler and warmer, like...like...'

'Like my apartment,' Vincenzo inserted softly when she floundered, seeing danger in what she had been about to say.

'As a matter of fact, I meant my mother's house!'

She didn't want to think of Vincenzo's apartment where she had spent the one, glorious, bitterly deluded night of her marriage. She had been delighted by it from the moment he had brought her there after their first meeting at the very beginning of her holiday. It had been full of light and warmth and, she had believed, love. She had thought it would be the home she would share with her husband after they had married.

'Your mother's house!' Vincenzo echoed savagely. 'The house I was never allowed to set foot inside. The mother I was never allowed to meet.'

'You were angry—furious!' Remembered horror darkened Amy's eyes at the thought. 'I'd have been a fool to let you anywhere near me.'

She could never tell him that she hadn't want to let him in because she had feared that if she did, then her home, her life in England, the one place that was free of any connection with the terrible mistake of her marriage, would be touched by his presence. If he once came inside, then she would always picture him there, and be haunted by the memory.

'And our marriage was over so there was no point in you ever meeting my mother—she was never going to be anything to you, nor you to her.'

'Our marriage was *not* over!'

'You lied to me!' Her voice was raw with pain that the passage of the intervening years had done nothing to ease. 'You never meant a word of your marriage vows.'

'I meant every word,' Vincenzo told her coldly. 'Till death do us part. *That* is why our marriage is not over. Why it will never be over!'

'What?'

Her head was spinning and she thought longingly of sinking down on the inviting comfort of the bed and closing her eyes. Pride alone kept her upright. Pride forced her to look into the inimical black depths of his eyes and see the molten steel of resolution that burned there, impervious to appeal.

'Never?'

An arrogant flick of one olive-skinned hand dismissed her shaken question.

'I am Italian, *cara*. Our religion forbids divorce. You know this. You knew it when you married me, and it still holds true today. In my book marriage is *per sempre*—for ever.'

'I...'

Words danced inside her head, but just out of reach. She couldn't focus her thoughts to catch any one of them or form them into a coherent sequence. And her confusion was made all the worse by the belated realisation that the arrogant hand Vincenzo had waved under her nose wore a ring on its wedding finger. A plain, broad band of gold that she herself had placed on it with such happiness on the morning of their wedding day.

Her own wedding ring was gone, she had no idea where. In the aftermath of the horror that had closed in around her the day after her marriage, she had flung it wildly at Vincenzo, refusing ever to wear it again. But he still had his. And it seemed that he planned to keep the commitment that went with it, despite the fact that his own actions had reduced that marriage to ashes from the first.

Which meant the sentence of death for all her own hopes of a future, of freedom, the real reason why she was here in the first place.

'You are my wife,' Vincenzo pronounced inflexibly. 'We may have been separated for four years, but nothing has changed that fact. You are back now—'

'*Vincenzo!*' Amy broke in, in desperation, all plans of revenge, of keeping him dangling, evaporating in the blaze of panic that fired in her mind.

She had to tell him. Had to get the truth out into the open. She couldn't continue this pretence any longer.

'Vincenzo, please!'

But even as she looked into his eyes again and saw there the same unyielding resolve as before, her nerve failed her.

'Please…' she began again, her voice quavering weakly. 'I'm tired—I'd really like to rest. Can—can we talk about this another time?'

His smile twisted in her heart like a cruel knife.

'But of course, *innamorata*. I told you, I can wait. But do not make me wait too long. I am not a patient man, and when I see how beautiful you have grown—'

'Oh, but…'

'Don't deny the truth,' Vincenzo growled, misinterpreting the reason for her protest. 'Four years ago you were a lovely young girl, poised on the edge of womanhood. But now that promise has been fulfilled. You are truly beautiful, Amy, even when you choose to hide that beauty in such unflattering clothes.'

Disdainful fingers flicked over the grey linen dress she wore, silent scorn implicit in the gesture. But even as Amy's lips formed a protest, he stilled for a moment and when he moved again the touch of his hands had changed, criticism turning to caress, severity to sensuality, in the space of a heartbeat.

'It is a crime to clothe skin as soft as this in dowdy colours.'

His voice had dropped, becoming warmly smoky, coiling round her senses in soft enchantment.

'To conceal the shape of your body in garments as stiff and uninviting as a suit of armour.'

Which was precisely why she had chosen this particular dress. But when Amy tried to force her tongue to frame the reply, she found it had frozen in her mouth, caught in the sensuous trap of his honeyed whisper. She wanted to break free from his touch, but, light as it was, it suddenly had all the power of a tempered steel chain.

'Amy, *cara mia*, we have already wasted too much time.'

'No…'

'*Yes.*' Vincenzo insisted, his dark head lowering slowly until his warm lips brushed her forehead. 'It doesn't have to be like this. Why should you fight when surrender would be so much sweeter?'

That tormenting mouth moved lower, pausing to caress her temples, her lowered eyelids, the high, slanting line of her cheekbones. Heat flooded her veins in an instant response, melting away the resistance she struggled to feel, weakening her hold on reality, making her head swim so that she swayed on unsteady feet.

Warm hands slid over her skin in the sleeveless dress, tracing the slender lines of her throat with a delicacy that had her arching into his touch like a contented cat responding to the stroke of its owner's hand. A heavy pulse was beating deep in the pit of her stomach, sending burning waves of response through the rest of her body, sensitising her nerves, dulling her senses of self-preservation and awakening the most primitive, most basic of needs she had ever known.

'Vincenzo…' she managed, her voice thick with an echo of the ache she felt inside, and heard his soft laughter in response.

'I know, *cara*. This is how it should be. This, and more…'

His mouth took hers in a kiss that seduced with its gentleness, numbing her thoughts and leaving her only capable of reacting. She returned the gentle pressure of his lips, the flare of hunger that seared through her adding an extra urgency to her kiss, her mouth opening under his, allowing the tantalising invasion of his tongue.

She hadn't felt him move, but suddenly she was enclosed in powerful arms, held close to the heat and hardness of his body, her pelvis crushed against the burning evidence of his fiercely aroused state. The world had contracted into a tiny microcosm in which there was nothing but herself and Vincenzo, no sense of anything but him, the musky scent of his skin in her nostrils, the tantalising play of his mouth on hers, the taste of his lips, the silken dance of his tongue.

In her ears was the crazy thunder of her own heart, the singing race of her blood in her veins. The heat of his palm burned through the fine material of her dress as his hand roughly cupped and caressed the aching swell of one breast, the other tangling in the dark fall of her hair, tilting her head backwards so that he could plunder her mouth further.

With knowing skill, he circled the pad of his thumbs over the hard, tight point of her nipple, and a sensation like the sear of an electric current licked its way along every nerve, centring in a pool of molten heat low down at the juncture of her thighs.

'Vincenzo...' she managed again, on a very different note this time. A low, keening, yearning sound that betrayed her soul just to hear it.

'Amy, *bellissima*!'

He sounded almost as shaken as she was, his voice rough and raw at the edges.

'Why did you do this to us? Why did you deny us this? Why did I? I shouldn't have let you get away from me. Well, never again, *moglie mia*, never again! This time, when I take you, I will hold you with me for ever. I will never let you go again.'

This time, when I take you... I will never let you go again...

The words slashed through the heated haze that clouded Amy's thoughts, snapping her back to reality with a speed and shock that made her stomach lurch queasily. Icy panic chilled her blood, killing the blazing heat and making the burning spiral of need tighten into a cold, hard knot of rejection.

'No-o-o.' It was a moan of confusion and fear as rational thought fought a nasty, bitter battle with stronger, more primitive instincts.

'*Si!*' Vincenzo's voice was insistent in her ear, the emphatic note making it plain that she was going to have to fight him as well as herself if she was to have any chance of winning. 'Yes, my wife.'

'No!'

That was better, it sounded stronger this time. Strong enough at least to still his wickedly caressing hands, inject a new, watchful tension into the powerful body that was crushed up against her own slender one.

'Vincenzo, *no*!' she tried again, desperately relieved to see that she had got through to him this time.

The hot kisses against her throat ceased and the proud dark head lifted, black eyes staring deep into her clouded blue ones, searching disbelievingly for the reasons for her unexpected reaction.

'Please—no…'

She didn't know if it was relief that made her voice wobble revealingly. Or, worse, something deeper and more secret that she didn't dare give a voice to.

'Vincenzo—I…I'm not ready for this.'

Thankfully, he accepted her clumsy explanation, taking only a few nerve-twisting seconds to adjust, straighten up, ease his hold on her. It all seemed to be done without the slightest degree of effort, but the way that he drew in his breath sharply, a distinct tremor in the hand he lifted to smooth the ruffled darkness of his hair told their own story. And when he spoke the rough edges still hadn't been smoothed from his deep tones.

'I understand. It is too early. The right moment will soon come.'

The right moment will never come! Hell would freeze over first.

The response screamed so loudly in Amy's thoughts that for one terrible moment she thought she had actually spoken them aloud. Vincenzo was perfectly capable of interpreting them as a challenge and turning on a full-scale charm assault in response.

And right now she was too shaken, too unnerved even to think of fighting back.

So she felt a wave of relief wash over her as Vincenzo let his hands fall to his sides.

'I will leave you to settle in. The drink you wanted will be sent up at once.'

Amy managed a vague murmur of response but any actual words were beyond her. She barely saw Vincenzo turn and stride from the room, concentrating hard on keeping a grip on herself, staying stiffly upright. But the slam of the door behind him took the last of her strength from her.

Sinking down onto the nearest chair, she let reaction swamp her, her heart pounding, her breathing fast and shallow. But mixed in with the urgent response of her senses was a terrible, aching sense of loss, of yearning for what couldn't be, what would never be. And the worst thing was that she knew exactly what had happened to her.

Sex. That summed up Vincenzo's behaviour and her own reaction to it in a single word. It was all about sex and nothing more. It was the way he had trapped her the last time, coiling his heated golden web around her and tangling her up in it so that she could never pull free.

Only then, four years before, so much younger and so foolishly naïve, she had blindly called it love. She had believed that the burning physical response she felt for Vincenzo, the forceful passion he made it plain he had for her, had everything to do with emotion and not just the more primitive, basic tug of lust. Now she knew better.

Sex and possession. Because mixed in with Vincenzo's obvious desire was the need to hold. To keep.

This time, when I take you... I will never let you go again.

She had always known that Vincenzo Ravenelli was a man to whom power and wealth was important. Already destined to inherit his father's fortune, he had set out to earn himself a second one in his own right. It seemed that everything he touched turned to gold—and everything he touched he *kept*, whether money, businesses, or people.

It was only after she had fled back home after her short-lived marriage that she had found out just how powerful Vincenzo actually was. Drawn by a masochistic impulse she couldn't control, she had been driven to read everything about him she could find.

She had learned of his reputation for wanting only the best, whether in his private life, or the things his companies produced. And that 'only the best' extended to his choice of the people who worked for him. A job with Ravenelli's was a job for life, David had told her. Because once Vincenzo got his hands on the ones he wanted, he never let them go.

David. The other man's name reminded her of the promise she had made to let her boss know where she was. She pulled her bag towards her, snatched out her cell phone and punched in the familiar number.

'Mr Brooke's office.' The crisp tones of David's temporary secretary, the one he had reluctantly agreed to employ while Amy herself was away, answered immediately.

'This is Amy Redman. Could I speak to David please?'

'I'm sorry, Miss Redman, but Mr Brooke is out of the office at the moment. But he said you might ring and asked me to take a message.'

'Oh…'

So what did she say? David believed she was on holiday. He had been none too pleased when she had announced that she needed to take time off at such short notice and had agreed to it only reluctantly. He wasn't the sort of man who was comfortable with impulsive decisions. He liked to build up to things slowly and carefully.

And just lately it had become obvious that he was slowly and carefully building up to asking her out. After three years of working for him, Amy was well used to her boss's every mood, so she couldn't miss the change in his attitude of late, the subtly dropped hints.

She didn't plan on acting on any of those hints. David wasn't her type at all. He was fine as a boss, but that was all. But his behaviour had made her look at her own life and forced her to question how long she was going to continue like this.

It was four years since she had left Vincenzo and in all that time she had avoided all other relationships, knowing that emotional complications were something she just couldn't handle. But perhaps now was the time to start thinking about rebuilding her life, beginning again. David might not be the man for her, but there might be others. But she couldn't even start to contemplate planning a future until she had sorted out the mess of the past.

And the first step towards doing that was seeing her husband and freeing herself from the shackles of her foolishly impulsive marriage.

'I promised to let him know that I'd arrived safely,' she said to the temporary secretary, recalling the scene in the office when David had insisted on her keeping in touch.

'You never know when I might need you,' he'd said. 'I don't trust these agency women.'

'And please could you tell him I'm going out tonight, so he might not be able to call me.'

The last thing she wanted was her phone ringing when she was with Vincenzo. This evening was going to be difficult enough without having to explain just who David was. And besides, Vincenzo had no right to know anything about the life she had made for herself in England.

Vincenzo was her past. At least, that was the way she had seen things going when she had set out to come to Venice in the first place. She knew she couldn't think of any sort of a future until she had freed herself from the travesty of her marriage. But Vincenzo's reaction had put paid to her dreams of a quick and easy escape from the long shadow he cast over her life.

In spite of the warmth of the afternoon, Amy shivered. She didn't have Vincenzo hooked at all. Instead, *he* had *her* trapped, able to grant her her freedom or withhold it from her on his slightest whim.

But she had come here to win that freedom. Without it she would have no hope of a future, no second chance at happiness. Somehow she had to persuade Vincenzo to let her go—but how?

CHAPTER THREE

TWENTY-FOUR hours later, Amy was nowhere nearer answering that question. And she was beginning to feel as if the golden web of seduction and power that had held her prisoner the first time was now enclosing her all over again.

It had started the night before in the moment that she had opened the wardrobe doors and discovered something that shocked her rigid.

Knowing that Vincenzo's family had always kept to the formality of dressing for dinner, she had cursed herself for not thinking to have packed something suitable. But then, of course, she had never anticipated staying in the Ravenelli home itself when she had decided to come to Venice. Foolishly, naively, she had imagined that she could call to see Vincenzo, explain why she was there, and then...

'And then what?' she asked herself out loud, frowning at her reflection in the ornate, gold framed mirror on the wall opposite the bed.

Had she truly believed that she would have told her husband that she wanted to end their marriage and he would say, 'Okay, fine, go right ahead?' That he would simply hold out his hands for the papers and meekly sign on the dotted line?

She had to have been dreaming if she had! The name 'Vincenzo Ravenelli' and the word 'meekly' were two things that could never be linked together in the same sentence—ever!

'So now what do I do?'

The only thing she could do was to keep her morale as high as it was possible. Put on the bravest face she could manage and try to find some way of pressing home the slightest advantage she could find.

And that being so, she wished she had brought something else to wear. While she had been downstairs with Vincenzo, one of the small army of staff her husband employed had come into the room and unpacked her belongings from the small canvas bag. So now Amy flung open the high, carved wooden doors of the huge wardrobe, expecting to see the few clothes she had brought with her looking pathetically insignificant in its cavernous depths.

What she did find made her heart jolt painfully, her breath catching sharply in her throat.

'I left almost all of my clothes behind.' She could hear her own voice flinging the words into Vincenzo's dark, proud face.

'And what makes you think that I kept them?' he had come back at her.

And yet now here she was staring in stunned disbelief at every item of clothing Vincenzo had ever bought her during those intense, sweet, heady days of their courtship, the few brief whirlwind weeks that had existed between the moment of their first meeting and the day that she had come to him as his bride.

'Oh, no!' It was a low, fearful moan, dragged from lips that were suddenly ashen with shock. 'Oh, no, no, no!'

She couldn't even begin to think what it might mean. Couldn't understand just why Vincenzo would want to hold on to her clothes, let alone have them stored with such care. Every garment had been cleaned and pressed to perfection, displayed under protective covering on beautifully padded hangers. The whole wardrobe looked as if she had just left it that way only that morning instead of never having been near it for four long years.

So it was no wonder that when, late into that long, dark, endless night, she finally fell asleep, she found that she had tumbled back into the past. In her dreams she was once again reliving her first visit to Venice, her meeting with Vincenzo and the fateful consequences that had resulted.

A month in Italy. It had seemed like the perfect twentieth birthday present. And one that she had sorely needed after the traumas and tribulations of the past six months. But at first, she had been reluctant to take the holiday.

'I couldn't leave you alone, Mum, not at a time like this. You need me.'

Sarah Redman had refused to take no for an answer.

'I have to start learning to live on my own sometime, darling! Besides, you need the break. You've done so much for me, these past six months. This is just my way of saying thank you. I'm proud of you and your—your father would be too.'

Amy couldn't suppress the scowl that the thought of her father always brought to her face these days. Six months before, like her mother, she had been devastated when Bill Redman had collapsed and died within minutes after a severe heart attack.

But what had followed afterwards had been so much worse. The discovery, at the funeral itself, that her father had had not only a mistress but also a second family, had shaken her to the core.

The betrayal of her mother had been bad enough. But what had shattered Amy's world had been the knowledge that her father's mistress had two other daughters, one almost exactly the same age as Amy herself. She had always known that her father had never really wanted children. Her own arrival had been an accident, one he had been determined never to repeat, but he had gone ahead and had a second child with the other woman in his life.

'I'll never forgive Dad for what he did to you—to both of us! He might just as well have said, "You don't matter—this is my real family."'

'It's done,' her mother had sighed. 'All the anger and regret in the world can't change a thing. But we can't let it blight our lives. We have to learn to live again and that's what this holiday is all about. I want to see you smile again. I want you to go to Italy and find a new life, new excitement, new friends.'

What she had found was Vincenzo.

Amy would never know what sort of malign fate had led her first to choose Venice as the starting point of her trip, and then to book into the hotel at which Salvatore Cristaldi was the deputy manager. From the start it had become clear that Sal was looking for something Amy wasn't. He had tried to get her into bed almost immediately, obviously believing that any single woman on holiday was looking for a 'no-strings' holiday affair.

But after that first date, Amy had found the initial effect of Sal's charm and good looks very soon wore off. If he didn't get what he wanted, he changed, becoming quite unpleasant in a way that made her feel he wasn't really to be trusted. She had had to express herself more forcefully than she was used to, to make it plain that she had no intention of sleeping with him.

And then Sal had introduced her to Vincenzo.

It had been like being at the mercy of a wild, tropical storm that had swept her off her feet, carried her along for days. And when she had finally set foot on the ground again it was to discover that nothing was as she remembered it, and would never be the same again.

"You haven't *married* her, have you?' Sal's voice echoed down through the years to torment her. '*Per Dio*, Cenzo! There was no need to go that far!'

If only Vincenzo had known that he needn't have married her to get what he wanted. By the time he had proposed, she had been so deeply in love with him, she would have given him anything. But at the beginning, still wounded by her father's betrayal, the way that it had made her feel, she had been too scared, too convinced that no man would stay with her if she let him make love to her.

And so she had held out, insisting that only marriage would get her into any man's bed.

And Vincenzo had seemed to understand. He had made it plain that he was as keen to make their relationship an intimate one as Sal had been, but he had also seemed to take her refusal much more easily, backing off when she had asked him to.

'I know how you're feeling,' he'd said one soft, warm evening as they travelled back to Venice after a day spent at the Lido. 'It can be frightening suddenly experiencing feelings like this when they're the last thing you're expecting. You meet someone who sets you back on your heels, rocks your whole existence, and you don't know how to handle it.'

'It's all happened so quickly,' Amy admitted.

Looking up into Vincenzo's jet-black eyes, she'd known why. From the moment that she'd first met him, she'd only wanted to be with him.

'And already more than half of my holiday is over,' she added, a raw note of pain shading her voice. 'Ten days from now...'

She couldn't go on. Tears flooded her eyes and she bent her head as she struggled to control them.

'I don't want to leave...'

'Then don't.'

Vincenzo's voice sounded almost as husky as her own, the warmth of his breath feathering over the sensitive coils of her ear as he bent his dark head close to hers.

'Stay here with me—as my wife.'

'Vincenzo!'

Amy's head came up sharply, deep-blue eyes wide with shock and disbelief as she stared into his strongly carved face.

'Vincenzo!' she said on a very different note. 'Don't do this; it's not fair! Don't tease me—because I know this isn't the truth. I can't believe...'

One long-fingered hand came under her chin, lifting her face so that her eyes met his.

'Believe it,' he said, his voice deepening on the words. 'Because I assure you, *cara mia*, that I never, ever lie—and certainly not about something like this. If I say I've never felt like this about any other woman, then that is the simple truth, nothing more, nothing less.'

'You...you mean it?'

'Every word,' he assured her huskily. 'I want you, Amy Redman. I want you more than any woman I've ever met. I was knocked off balance in the moment I first saw you and I've never been able to concentrate on anything but you since. I want you so much that I can't sleep, can't work. My hunger for you is like an ache that torments me day and night until I think I'll go crazy if you leave me. I know it's too soon—we hardly know each other—but I don't think I can let you go back to England and out of my life.'

From that moment on she had been caught up in a whirlwind of excitement and happiness that had made every day like living in a dreamworld. She hadn't even queried Vincenzo's insistence that they have a small private wedding, as soon as possible, seeing it as just one more romantic touch in what was already a fairytale come true.

They could tell their families and friends later, he had assured her. Have a big society reception where everyone could meet up after the event. For now, the ceremony would be just the two of them and a couple of witnesses.

And, drifting along on a cloud of happiness, Amy had agreed to everything he had said. She was marrying the most wonderful man in the world, in the most beautiful city in the world, and that was all that mattered. She knew her mother would understand and be happy for her.

The bubble of happiness that had enclosed her had lasted for just a few more days. She had floated through the wedding, the intimate meal that had followed. Her wedding night had been everything she had ever dreamed off—more than that. Vincenzo had been the perfect lover, ardent, hotly passionate, yet so very considerate of her feelings, her enjoyment that the loss of her virginity had been nothing more than small discomfort, forgotten instantly in the ecstasy that followed.

She had drifted off to sleep in state of total bliss, wrapped tightly in Vincenzo's arms, held close against the warm strength of his muscled body. She had had a long, dreamless night and had woken full of joy, anticipating the first of many long, contented days ahead of her, the rest of her married life.

It had taken just one hour to disillusion her completely.

Some small sound had disturbed her; she had no idea what. Yawning heavily, and rubbing the sleep from her eyes, Amy frowned a little as she realised that she was alone in the bed. When she had drifted asleep, Vincenzo had been lying beside her; long, bronzed limbs tangled with hers, heavy eyelids drooping over eyes that were hazed by sensual satisfaction.

But now Vincenzo had left her, and she was anxious to find him again. Without his warm body close beside her, the big bed felt empty and strangely unwelcoming. She needed to find her husband, see his eyes light up as he opened his arms for her to go into them like a small, contented, homing bird.

Sounds from the living room drew her there, frowning in confusion as she heard two voices, blurred as a result of the closed door. Vincenzo's and another that was vaguely familiar.

'Cenzo?'

The first surprise was that Vincenzo had taken the time to put on his clothes. Unlike Amy herself, who had only pulled on a thin, silky robe, the colour of rich clotted cream, over her naked body, he was now fully dressed in oatmeal-

coloured trousers and a softly clinging T-shirt in the tones
of milky coffee.

The second shock was the identity of the person with
him. Amy had never expected to see Salvatore with his
cousin, and she felt distinctly uncomfortable at appearing
in only the thin, clinging robe. Her discomfort was added
to by the obvious amusement in Sal's eyes, the lingering,
almost salacious survey he subjected her to, bringing a rush
of burning colour into her cheeks.

'*Buon giorno*, Amy.' He greeted her, his smile growing
at her obvious consternation. 'I see you have been making
my cousin a very happy man.'

'I…Cenzo?'

Confused and unsure of how to proceed, Amy looked to
Vincenzo for help, surprised to find that instead of the
warmly affectionate welcome she had expected, his features
were set in an expression of watchful distance, his black
eyes revealing no emotion whatsoever. Uneasily she pulled
the cream robe closer around her slim body, tightening the
belt at her waist.

'I came round to congratulate him as soon as I realised.'

'Sal.' Vincenzo's deep voice sounded a note of warning
and suddenly everything seemed to make sense to Amy.

'Congratulate…Cenzo, you told him!'

She was torn between relief and reproach. Vincenzo had
promised that they would tell his family together; that he
wouldn't say a word until she was there with him. But at
least if Sal's reaction was in any way typical then she had
no need to be afraid about the way the news would be
received. She had been haunted by a lingering fear that the
Ravenelli family would disapprove violently of their hasty
marriage, seeing her as a gold-digger who couldn't wait to
get her hands on a wealthy man.

'Told me!' Sal's amusement was even more pronounced.
'Amy, sweetheart, it wasn't a matter of *telling* me. I'd have
to be blind to miss the evidence. The fact that your key

was still at reception at the hotel was a major clue. The way your bed hadn't been slept in, another.'

'Sal, that's enough,' Vincenzo growled, but his cousin was unstoppable.

'I'm sure you know you've made Vincenzo's day,' Sal went on, his smile wide and bright in a way that was beginning to grate on Amy's nerves. 'But I wonder if you know just how much you've done for him? Still, I'm sure he'll be only too pleased to show his gratitude, won't you, Cenzo?'

'I said, that's *enough*!'

When Vincenzo used that tone, Amy was surprised to find that Sal hadn't turned to stone where he stood. Even loving him as she did, she still flinched inside when he snapped out a command like that, her blood running suddenly cold in apprehension. But Sal appeared completely uncowed.

'No need for embarrassment, cousin!' he returned blithely. 'You won, fair and square, I'll admit it. And to prove I'm a man of my word…'

Pushing a hand into his pocket, he pulled out something small enough to hold completely in his palm, his fingers closed around it.

'Here…'

He tossed it towards Vincenzo who managed to catch it one-handed, in spite of the fact that all his attention was centred totally on Amy's face, polished onyx eyes locking with confused and shadowed blue ones.

She was suddenly, disturbingly, shockingly aware of just how little she knew about this man who was now her husband. She had given him her heart, her body, she knew she would give him her soul if he asked for it, but she could never claim that she really knew him. And looking at him now, seeing icy withdrawal where she had expected warmth and love, she felt as if she was in the presence of a total stranger.

'V-Vincenzo…'

She needed the length of his full name to get her voice to work, no longer feeling free to use the shortened, more affectionate form.

'What's happening?'

Still with his eyes locked with hers, Vincenzo lifted the hand that held the small box Sal had tossed to him. With it resting on the flat of his palm, he held it out to her.

'I want you to have this.'

'*Cenzo!*'

Sal's exclamation was a croak of shock and sheer blank disbelief.

'Cenzo, what the devil are you doing? You can't give that to *her.*'

A muscle tugged faintly of the corner of Vincenzo's mouth, creating something that might have been a smile, but was there and gone before it registered.

'Amy…' he said, ignoring his cousin, all attention centred on her face.

Slowly, automatically, totally unable to think for herself, Amy moved forward, her actions like those of a sleep-walker, looking neither to right or to left. As she came closer, Vincenzo opened the box with a flick of his hand and pulled out the ring it contained. With his free hand he reached for hers, the one that bore the wedding ring he had placed on it only the day before.

'I never bought you an engagement ring…' he murmured huskily. 'Perhaps this will compensate.'

All Amy's breath escaped her in a gasp of shock as she looked down and saw the fabulous ring he was pushing on to her finger. In the middle of an ornate, beautifully intricate gold setting a huge ruby gleamed, its burnished colour like the glow at the centre of a fire.

'Cenzo!' she breathed in awe. 'It's fabulous!'

'Vincenzo!' Sal's shocked voice broke into her stunned

delight. '*Cugino*, what the hell are you doing? You *can't* give the Ravenelli ruby—'

Vincenzo's head snapped round, something dangerous flaring deep in the black eyes.

'I can give what I like to my wife.'

'Your… Oh, *Dio! Cenzo…*'

Coming forwards hastily, Sal caught hold of his cousin's arm, turning him away from Amy, his dark head bent conspiratorially towards his cousin's.

'Cenzo, tell me it isn't true. You haven't *married* her, have you? There was no need to take it that far. I mean, I would have paid out on our bet if you'd simply bedded her. You didn't have to sign your life away.'

'Bet… What..?'

Amy was struggling to take in a word of this bewildering conversation.

'Cenzo, you're not saying you had a *bet* on…on…'

She couldn't form the words; they were too dreadful, too frightening. But they were there, in her head, like some appalling scream of pain and fear.

'Vincenzo?'

'Yes.'

It was like the cut of a brutal knife. Hard and stark and totally destructive. It slashed into the dream world that had enclosed her, ripping it into pieces and destroying it forever, letting a terrible reality in to shatter her.

'I…' Sal began but Vincenzo turned on him, eyes blazing.

'Sal—get out!'

'But…'

'*Per Dio*, I said get out!' Vincenzo roared with a ferocity that even his cousin wouldn't dare risk stirring any further.

As the door slammed behind him Vincenzo turned back to Amy, launching into a harsh, emotionless explanation.

'Sal and I had a bet. He said there was this girl—a stunning, fabulous girl who he wanted so badly he thought he would die—but she would have nothing to do with him. He bet me—'

'That even you couldn't get me into bed,' Amy's voice was a dull, bruised monotone of disbelief. 'That even your very special seduction techniques wouldn't work on this one.'

Even as she spoke the awful truth she couldn't yet accept, she was praying that somehow Vincenzo would make it right. That he would deny her appalling interpretation and give her another one entirely. One that would heal the anguish deep inside, restore her faith in this man who was her husband.

But he didn't.

'That's about right,' he said flatly. 'And the stake was...'

Amy looked down at her hand. At the ring that burned on her finger, looking to her agonised mind for all the world like a great, ominous drop of blood welling from some incurable wound.

'The Ravenelli ruby.'

'Yes.'

Vincenzo didn't even have the grace to look guilty, ashamed, or even the slightest touch embarrassed. Instead, those cold, hard onyx eyes regarded her shocked, bloodless face, and the navy-blue bruises that were her eyes with a steady confidence that rocked her sense of reality.

Totally secure in his supreme male arrogance, it was obvious that he didn't even feel that what he had done might be wrong. That direct, unwavering gaze showed no sign of understanding the agony of betrayal he had subjected her to.

This couldn't be happening! She had to have fallen asleep and tumbled, unaware, into the most terrifying, most appalling nightmare of her life. At any moment she would wake up and discover that this had never really happened.

But Vincenzo had said that her suspicions were well founded; the horror was true.

And Vincenzo never lied.

In another part of her brain she could hear Vincenzo's own words when he had told her the story of the Ravenelli ruby. It had been in the family for centuries until Vincenzo's grandfather had lost it to his hated brother-in-law—Sal's grandfather—from whom Sal himself had recently inherited it.

'He doesn't even value it,' Vincenzo had told her. 'He has no time for anything old, any tradition. But for years his family has refused any offer we've made to try and buy it back.'

'And why is it so special to you?'

'That ring should have been my mother's. My father should have given it to her on their wedding day, just as my grandfather should have given it to my grandmother. That has always been the tradition. A tradition that had been kept unbroken until my grandfather pledged it on the gaming tables. I would give the world to be able to restore that tradition—do anything at all to get it back.'

Her stomach lurched nauseously, the bitter taste of acid in her mouth. Somehow she found the strength to force herself to speak.

'Well, I hope that one night we spent together was worth it, because that's all you're going to get.'

With fingers that shook so hard she could hardly force them to grip, she wrenched the ring from her finger and flung it straight in his face. Just to touch it seemed to send shockwaves of distress up her arm, made her feel as if some terrible corruption had entered her blood, contaminated her soul.

Her wedding ring followed. She could barely watch its progress as it hit Vincenzo's broad shoulder and bounced off, landing on the floor somewhere and rolling away. Her eyes were blurred with burning, agonising tears that she resolutely refused to let fall.

Dragging up a strength she didn't know she had, she dug

deep inside the pain that was all that possessed her, needing something, anything at all, to hit back with. All she knew was the hurt he had inflicted on her. That and the need to throw it right back at him. To make him know some tiny part of what she was going through.

'It appears we each had our own private agenda going into this marriage. And, luckily it seems to have worked out for both of us.'

'Worked out?'

He hadn't expected attack, that much was obvious. The jet eyes were wary now, his expression, his whole stance watchful and alert.

'That's right.'

She astounded herself by being able to produce a nonchalant little shrug, even flashing a dismissive smile on and off, like a brilliant neon sign.

'You wanted the ruby. I wanted a rich husband. Oh, you didn't believe that "love at first sight" garbage did you? Well, I'm sorry to disappoint you, but my motives were far more…'

She made a play of hunting for the right word.

'Practical.'

'You mercenary bitch!'

'And that's very definitely the filthy pot calling the grubby kettle black!'

This time her anger was genuine, her head coming up, blue eyes flashing fury at his hypocrisy.

'You were playing for much the same stakes, yourself.'

At least he had the grace not to deny it this time. She wouldn't have been able to bear it if he had argued with her, tried to convince her otherwise.

'Oh, Vincenzo, darling,' she mocked gently, determined to give another twist to the knife in case he was thinking of coming up with some explanation she might just have to listen to, be tempted to consider or believe. 'You don't really believe that I slept with you simply out of desire, do you?'

When he gave no answer, regarding her with the coldest, hardest eyes she had ever seen, she swallowed deeply and forced herself to go on.

'The desire I can't deny. I'd be a fool to try. But I needed your wedding ring on my hand if I was to have any claim on my rights as your wife. But then, of course, you'd understand that. I expect you and Sal came up with much the same sort of conditions over the ruby.'

'Get out.'

It was nothing like the way he had spoken to Sal. Instead, it was a low, menacing whisper, brimming with a danger that made her shiver convulsively.

'Get out of my sight. If I ever see you again it will be too soon.'

She had taken him at his word. She had fled to the bedroom, flinging her few belongings back into the case she had barely unpacked the night before, and escaping from the apartment without ever seeing her husband. And when he'd followed her to England, she'd taken the greatest satisfaction in slamming her mother's door in his face.

CHAPTER FOUR

'ARE you ready?'

Vincenzo's voice interrupted her memories of the previous night, jarring her back to the present with an uncomfortable jolt. Blinking dazedly, she saw the polished jet gaze focus on her sharply, sweeping from the top of her shining dark head, over the simple, flowing lines of her dress to the toes of her low-heeled patent pumps in a swift, assessing survey before he gave a small, unsmiling nod of satisfaction.

'I'm glad you decided on the red,' he murmured, his tone soft as velvet. 'I always liked you in that.'

'Well you needn't think I chose this dress to please you!' Amy retorted with tart defiance, her chin coming up, blue eyes flashing in refutation of even the thought.

'Of course not.'

The deliberate irony, the obvious implication that in fact he meant the exact opposite, aggravated Amy's already decidedly edgy mood, so that she had to grit her teeth against the furious outburst that almost escaped her. It didn't help that every sense in her own body was unnervingly already on red alert in response to the sensual appeal of Vincenzo's lean, strong body in the black informal suit that screamed Italian styling in every tailored inch, a pale blue V-necked T-shirt clinging to the hard lines of his chest, exposing the tanned column of his throat.

'As you know very well, I only brought the basic minimum with me,' she managed, her jaw stiff and tight, her lips feeling frozen so that she could hardly get the words out. 'I didn't expect to be dining with you or spending the day out sightseeing.'

'*Naturalmente.*' The low murmur was even more sardonic, the faint flicker of a smile mocking her indignation, incensing her further.

'What I brought with me was only enough for a day or so. My dress was crumpled after the flight—'

'You do not have to explain,' Vincenzo inserted smoothly. 'No woman should ever need to justify choosing a dress that brings out her true beauty over one that makes her look like some dowdy secretary.'

'As a matter of fact, a secretary is exactly what I am!'

Amy took a rather perverse delight in tossing the declaration at him, seeing the way his face changed, the beautiful mouth thinning harshly, black eyes narrowing in angry assessment.

'You don't like that, do you?' she taunted when he seemed uncharacteristically at a loss for words. 'You really don't like to think of me earning my living at all. What is it, Vincenzo? Is it the idea of my lowly station that appals you? The thought that you, a Ravenelli of Venice, should be tied to someone who actually earns their living in such a menial capacity? Someone who...'

'If you want to know the truth, then what *appals* me is that you should work for anyone at all!' Vincenzo inserted coldly, his voice rough with dark anger. 'That you, my wife, should work for some man who would watch you, lust after you, think thoughts about you that he has no right to.'

So this was what really troubled him, Amy reflected bitterly. The deeply jealous, possessive Vincenzo Ravenelli hated the thought of her associating with any other man, even if just to work for him. He didn't love her himself, but that didn't stop him wanting to *own* her, control her life. She was his wife, and what he had he kept.

This time, when I take you... I will never let you go again.

Sex and possession. Just the sound of the words in her thoughts made Amy shiver in apprehension.

'And besides,' Vincenzo continued still in that low, black-edged tone, 'there was no need for you to work at all. You were well provided for. The allowance I made you—'

'I didn't want your allowance! I wouldn't have touched it if I was derelict and starving in a gutter! I would rather have swept the streets than take your money, Vincenzo! I can't be bought that way!'

'I had no intention of *buying* you! That money was yours, by right, as my wife.'

'Your *wife*!'

The burn of agony deep inside put a savagery into her voice that simple anger could never have created.

'I was never your wife, Vincenzo! I was only a passing fancy, a plaything—something you saw, and wanted, like a child who screams and screams until they get the latest fashionable toy, and then discards it only hours later when they've tired of it.'

'And what makes you think I have tired of you?' It came swift and low, with the force of a striking snake. 'You do yourself an injustice, *innamorata,* if you truly believe that the appeal of your charms can pall after just one night. It is precisely because I am still hungry for you that I was prepared to tolerate your foolish behaviour.'

'And precisely what "foolish behaviour" might that be?' Amy demanded, deliberately lacing her tone with acid.

'Your childish temper-tantrum when you discovered that our marriage was not quite the perfect fairy story you had concocted in your juvenile fantasies. The way you ran home to mother without waiting for any explanation or the truth—'

'The *truth*, if I recall rightly, was that you married me not for myself but for something very much more mundane—the price of a damn ring!'

'The Ravenelli ruby could never be described as mundane,' Vincenzo tossed back at her, supremely indifferent to her distress. 'To my family it has a value beyond accounting. It is priceless.'

'Priceless? Is that what you call it? So tell me, Signor Ravenelli, is anything, anything at all, of more value than a human heart? Is any possession, however old, however beautiful, worth the cost of destroying another person's happiness, of taking it and trampling it underfoot?'

'I gave you what you wanted. I married you. You had my ring on your finger, my name. You had my wealth— "All that I have I share with you."'

Cynically he quoted from the wedding vows he had made. The vows that had once made her heart soar and sing in delight but now had acquired a terrible, bitter twist that stabbed straight to her soul.

'You still have all of those. What more could you want?'

His love. All that she had ever wanted was his love, and, without that, nothing had any value. She hadn't cared about his famous name or his stunning wealth. If he had been the poorest man in the whole of Italy, but he had loved her, it would have been enough.

'L...' she began but fear closed her throat over the word and she couldn't say it. 'Nothing so cold,' she choked out. 'What about feeling? What about passion?'

'Passion? Oh, Amy, *cara*. There was always passion. There still is. It was you who insisted on marriage and it was a price I was prepared to pay. I still am.'

'I...'

Once more her voice failed her, the rush of her memories swamping her thoughts. The appalling thing was that she couldn't deny him, couldn't fling a furious rejection of his dreadful words straight into his smug, sardonically smiling face, no matter how much she might dream of doing so.

She *had* insisted on marriage. Had refused to take their relationship any further, refused to go to bed with him,

without the degree of commitment a wedding ring implied.
Emotionally battered and bruised by the events of the past
six months, shocked to the core by the discoveries she had
made about her father, the destruction of all she had believed to be true, she had needed so much more than just
a casual fling. And so she had held out for marriage or
nothing.

And the terrible, savage irony was that the precious wedding ring had meant so much less than any casual sexual
affair might have done. At least an affair would have been
more open, more honest; it would have stated its terms, so
to speak, up front from the start. She had thought that all
her dreams had come true when Vincenzo had asked her
to marry him. It was only later, when she had realised exactly *why* he had done so, that the devastating deception he
had practised on her had hit home.

'And what if I don't want this marriage to continue?'

His smile turned her blood to ice, made her heart struggle
to beat.

'I told you, *carissima*, that is not an option.'

'But surely you would prefer to be free—to marry
again?'

'*You* are my wife.' It was harsh, inflexible, totally unyielding. A death knell to all her hopes of a future.

'But…but what if you fell in love?'

'Love?'

His accent had deepened, thickened on the single word,
turning it into a syllable of total disbelief. He sounded as
if he had no understanding at all of what the word meant,
as if he had been unaware of its existence until now.

'And you must want children.'

'I always assumed that any children I had would have
you as their mother.'

It was like the stab of a stiletto going straight to her
unprotected heart. She had wanted his babies, too. Had
dreamed, even before her wedding night, of a small son or

daughter with Vincenzo's black hair and eyes. She wouldn't have cared if that first night together had left her pregnant, so hungry had she been to hold his child in her arms.

'It seems to me, Vincenzo, that you made too many *assumptions* in the past. Perhaps if you'd stopped to consider anyone else's needs, you might not have made such a mess of things—'

'And perhaps if you had paused to consider anyone's needs other than your own, then you might not have been so very blind,' Vincenzo inserted with a smooth arrogance that literally took her breath away, leaving her gasping like a stranded fish. 'It seems to me that you were far less unhappy with the arrangement than you pretended to be.'

'Pretended!'

Amy couldn't believe what she was hearing. Had he really believed her tears, her distress, the agony of heartbreak he had put her through, had all been nothing but a *pretence*?

'Well, you were only too eager to tell me you'd married me for my money four years ago—and it seems that the idea of wearing a token of my esteem now is still not repugnant to you.'

'I told you—I didn't bring any other clothes with me!'

How she wished she hadn't succumbed to feminine vanity after all! She should have known just what an interpretation Vincenzo would put on what had seemed just a practical course of action.

'I had no choice, so—'

'It was not your clothes I was thinking of.'

The sudden movement of his eyes, the way the dark gaze dropped from hers, homing in on a point at the base of her neck dried the words in her mouth as she hastily reconsidered. With an uncomfortable little judder of her heart she realised just what he was looking at.

Instinctively her hands flew up to touch the fine gold

chain, shaking fingers closing over the single, beautifully cut diamond that hung from it.

If the truth were told, she had forgotten she was wearing the necklace, its delicacy making it almost weightless around her throat. It had been the first gift Vincenzo had given her on the day of their engagement, the most simple piece of jewellery he had presented her with, and always her favourite. She had never taken it off from the moment he had fastened it around her neck until the day when, her eyes blurred by bitter tears, she had left it behind along with everything else he had given her.

Last night, finding it in a box on her dressing table, she had been unable to resist trying it on. It had settled into its accustomed place with an ease and familiarity that had torn at her heart, bringing bittersweet memories rushing to the surface of her thoughts. She had fully intended to replace it where she had found it, but sleep had claimed her before she had done so. And this morning she had simply not noticed it was there, slipping back into past patterns without even realising that she had done so.

'You promised me a diamond for every year of our marriage!' she flung at Vincenzo now, using attack to disguise the sudden vulnerability that clawed at her painfully.

'So I did.' Smooth as ever, he didn't miss a beat. 'So now I owe you another four. If you will let me have it...'

'Oh, no!'

Thoroughly unnerved, Amy struggled to ignore his outstretched hand. To give him the necklace now, to allow him even to think of adding other jewels to the single, perfect stone, would seem to be colluding in his determination that their marriage was to last; that she was never to be free from him.

'You don't want the stones?'

The cold-eyed questioning gaze he slanted in her direction shrivelled her protest on her tongue.

'What woman would be fool enough to turn down diamonds?'

She aimed for airy flippancy and was pleased to find she almost hit it, just a touch of brittleness marring the effect.

'But we're late enough already. If we delay any longer, the day will be half over before we've even set foot outside. And you did promise me a tour of the city.'

When he had suggested the idea this morning over breakfast, she had snatched at it gratefully, thankful for the thought of some way to fill the long hours of the day. If Vincenzo was set on staying away from his office—and she knew the determined set of his handsome features well enough to realise that she had no hope at all of persuading him to change his mind—then she preferred to be out and about. That way at least she could dilute the potent impact of his forceful personality with the bustle and noise of the city at large. And besides, she had always adored Venice.

She had fallen in love with the city from the moment that she had first set foot there, and the thought that she might get another chance to explore this most beautiful of places was an unexpected delight. When she had set out for Italy, this time, she had believed that she would have no chance to linger, that she would have to declare the reason for her visit and then leave at once.

But Vincenzo's unexpected reaction to her appearance and her own fearful lack of the courage needed to explain just why she was here had at least allowed an unexpected bonus in this sightseeing trip.

'So I did.'

Vincenzo lifted his broad shoulders in a shrug of resigned acceptance.

'If that is what you want, then that is what we'll do. So if you're ready, *cara*?'

The first surprise was his easy agreement, his willingness to go along with what she wanted. It made the prospect of the whole day seem somehow brighter, easier, so that Amy actually found herself relaxing in his company. The second surprise was one that had her mouth opening wide in shock, a gasp of disbelief escaping her.

'A gondola, Vincenzo!' she exclaimed when she saw the form of transport he had laid on for them. 'You shouldn't have!'

On her first visit to Venice she had stared longingly at the elegant boats that were always associated in everyone's minds with the essence of Venice, knowing that her meagre allowance wouldn't run to the cost of hiring one even for an hour.

'Nothing but the best for my wife.' Vincenzo dismissed her protest with a snap of his fingers as he handed her into the swaying craft and settled her against the cushioned seat before coming to lounge beside her in elegant indolence. 'Today will be perfection from start to finish.'

And the final surprise was that that perfection was exactly the word Amy would have used to describe the experience. With only bitter, painful memories of lies and betrayal uppermost in her mind she had forgotten how, when he set his mind to it, Vincenzo could turn on an overwhelming charm that was positively lethal to any weakly susceptible female heart.

And today had been a small reminder of just how effective that charm could be, Amy reflected as the afternoon sunshine began to fade and the gondola made its way through the canals back towards Vincenzo's home. It was as if, in their mutual enjoyment of the day, and Vincenzo's evident delight in sharing his love of this beautiful city, some sort of a truce had been declared.

'Happy?' Vincenzo had caught her sigh and recognised it for the sound of content that it was.

'Very.'

She didn't have to struggle to inject a genuine enthusiasm into her voice and the smile that she directed up into his watchful dark gaze was warm and unrestrained.

'I've had a lovely day. In fact, there's just one thing missing. One thing that would make it quite perfect.'

'Let me guess…'

Vincenzo's own smile in response was knowing, very slightly complacent.

'Dinner and *bellinis* at Harry's Bar…' A slight inclination of his head acknowledged her start of surprise. 'I anticipated that. I know my wife.'

And he had been the one to introduce her to the particular mixture of champagne and peach juice to which she had become hopelessly addicted.

'The table is booked for nine. All you have to do is to dress—to make yourself look even more beautiful than you do now—and I will do the rest.'

When he smiled like that, the past four years melted away. That smile gave her back the man she had once known, if not the man she had loved.

And he was still the sexiest man she had ever met in her life. The bitter knowledge of the monstrous way he had treated her, the way he'd used her, had done nothing to dilute the stunning impact of glossy black hair and the deepest, darkest eyes she'd ever seen. With him lounging here beside her, long, powerful legs stretched out in front of him, the sinking sun gilding smooth, olive skin to molten gold, the clean male scent of his body tantalising her nostrils, she knew she had only been half alive until today. Knew that no man had ever touched her senses, brought them into singing response as fast and as easily as he could.

And she also knew that she had been lying when she had allowed him to believe that simply dinner at Harry's Bar and a cocktail was all that she needed to make her day complete.

What she wanted was far more basic and primitive than that.

And far more dangerous.

It was impossible to keep her clouded blue gaze from

going to Vincenzo's mouth and lingering, refusing to be dragged away again. Impossible not to trace the finely carved shape of his upper lip with her eyes, then take a slow, sensual survey of the softer, fuller curve of the lower one. Impossible not to think of that mouth pressed against her own in a long, demanding kiss. The heady combination of the hard and the soft, enticement and demand. And she knew that that was what she wanted most in all the world.

Kiss me, Vincenzo!

The words were so loud, so clear inside her head that she couldn't believe she hadn't actually said them.

And yet something had alerted Vincenzo anyway.

Something about her face, her expression, the truth he could read in her eyes. Something about the inclination of her body, turned instinctively towards his like the pointer on a compass automatically seeking true North. Something silent and unspoken, but communicating on the deepest, most intuitive level between two human beings so that words were unnecessary, superfluous.

'Amy…' he said and her name was a sound of enticement, a caress in itself.

She didn't know which one of them moved first. Whether her head lifted towards his or his lowered all in the same moment. All she was aware of was Vincenzo and his arms coming round her, his lips coming closer. The warm touch of the sun, the faint sound of the water, the sway of the boat as it slid forwards under the impulse of the gondolier's movement faded into a buzzing blur as their mouths met after what seemed like an endless agony of waiting.

And it was his gentleness that stunned her most. When she had expected the heated passion, the cruel demand of the previous afternoon, the delicacy, the tenderness of this caress took her breath away.

Her heart clenched in sharp response, hot tears stung her eyes and slid out from under the corners of her closed lids and she gave herself up to feeling, to need, to the sheer, burning joy of achieving her heart's desire.

'Amy...' Vincenzo murmured against her mouth, his voice thickened and rough. *'Carissima. Bella mia.'*

His hands were in her hair, tangling in the dark silky strands as he held her closer, keeping her mouth against his so that he could take it, taste it to his heart's content. And still with that same stunning gentleness, with a lightness of touch that she could have broken free of in a second if she only exerted the slightest effort.

But that effort was beyond her. She didn't have the focus of mind, never mind the strength, to move, to even think of doing anything other than simply respond. Her mouth opened under his, her lips parting to allow the silken invasion of his tongue, every nerve, every cell in her body tingling into life as if a fizzing electrical current had set them all alight.

She had lost all awareness of where she was, who she was. She only knew that this...

'Signore...'

The careful cough, the single word, polite and softly spoken as it was, still had the effect of an icy blade slicing through the glow of contentment that held her where she was.

'Signor Ravenelli...'

It was only the gondolier, politely hesitant, informing them that they had reached their destination, but it shattered the world that had enclosed them, bringing reality rushing back with a vengeance.

With a cry of shock Amy started back, shadowed blue eyes opening wide in distress, clouding in disbelief at what had just happened.

'I...' she began, but Vincenzo's low-toned laughter killed the words on her lips.

'Oh Amy, Amy,' he chided softly. 'There is no need to look as if the world has come to an end. It was just a kiss.'

Just a kiss. Just a kiss. The phrase beat at Amy's temples until she was ready to scream, fighting against the impulse to lift her hands and press them against her skull in an attempt to drive the tormenting words away.

Just a kiss. No, it had been so much more than that. For Vincenzo it might just have been a casual caress, but her own response had brought home to her the truth of the terrible danger she was in. A danger that came as much from herself as from any action Vincenzo might take.

And that danger could only grow and grow with every second she spent in Italy, in Vincenzo's home. She had to break free, get away once and for all—and stay away. Only then would she be safe.

She would have to tell Vincenzo the truth and she would have to do it tonight. She could only pray that dinner at Harry's Bar might just mellow him enough to listen to her without shooting her down in flames, because she didn't dare to leave it any longer than that.

CHAPTER FIVE

'ARE you tired?'

Vincenzo's low-toned question broke into Amy's absorbed thoughts, making her start in shock and turn wide, uncertain eyes on his shadowed face as he paused just outside the pool of light shed by the nearest street lamp.

'Should I not have dismissed the water taxi?'

'No...'

Fearful that the way she had shaken her head, sending the dark strands of her hair flying around her face, might have seemed over-emphatic, far too emotional, that it might draw his attention to her in a way she dreaded, she switched on what she hoped was a believable smile.

'No, really, I'm fine.'

She would have to do better than that if she was to convince him there was nothing wrong. Already those deep eyes were searching her face, probing with a laser-like intensity for the truth behind the careful act she was showing him.

She couldn't bear it if he so much as suspected that her steps had slowed, her feet dragging, because she wanted to delay as much as possible the moment when they would reach his house. The moment when the hesitation she had allowed herself must come to an end, and she must tell him the real reason why she was here in Italy at all.

'It's just that—that everywhere looks so lovely in the moonlight...'

Her gesture took in the high, full moon, the gently lapping waters of the canal, the houses on the opposite bank painted in amazing spicy colours of saffron yellow and turmeric red, the ornate, decorated pillars of the street lamp with its triple lights high above her head.

'I just want to take it all in.'

Take it in and store it in her mind against the future that now seemed to be rushing in on her so fast, well before she was quite ready to face it.

The whole evening had had an unbelievable, dreamlike quality about it, so that she felt she had been living in a bubble of time, suspended from reality. From the moment she had left her bedroom, dressed for dinner at Harry's Bar in a slim-fitting sleeveless deep purple velvet dress topped by a matching evening coat, to find Vincenzo waiting for her, dark and devastating in a black suit, severe white shirt and silver-grey tie, she had been able to let herself forget the past and live only in the present.

Or perhaps what she really meant was that she had let herself slip back into the further past, into the time before reality had hit home and she had learned the truth about the reasons why this man had made her his wife. It was as if those terrible, tearing moments of disillusionment and distress had never been.

She was once more the Amy Redman who had never known the shocking force and power of love at first sight. Never experienced the sense of being blasted out of a world she knew and into one where everything had splintered into tiny pieces and been replaced in a new and very different way, one she didn't recognise at all.

And Vincenzo was the sophisticated, charming, delightful companion who lit up her life simply by being in it. The man whose personality shone like the brightest star, who concentrated his attention on her with an intensity that took her breath away, making her feel as if she was the only woman in a world in which no one else existed.

And so, after dinner when he had suggested that they dismiss their water taxi near the Rialto Bridge and complete the rest of their journey home on foot, she had accepted willingly. This way the trip back would take so much longer. She could even delude herself, just for the moment, that the evening would never have to come to an end. That she would never have to look into the darkness of those coal-black eyes and watch them change, icing over, as she asked him for a divorce.

'I mean, have you ever seen anything so beautiful?'

'Never.'

Vincenzo's voice was suddenly husky, strangely raw, and when Amy looked up at him in confusion it was to meet the full force of those amazing eyes, find them fixed on her face with a fierce concentration that made her heart clench inside her chest.

'No, *cara mia*, I have never seen anything so beautiful in my life. And we both know that I am not talking about the moon or the damn canal, but about you.'

Reaching out, he took hold of her wrist, drawing her slowly but irresistibly forwards into the light of the street lamp. And there was nowhere she could look but into his strongly carved face, its planes and features thrown into sharp relief, the slash of his cheekbones, the dark pools of his eyes accentuated by the fall of the moonlight.

'I have waited so long for this moment that I cannot truly believe it is real. That you are here, back with me, where you belong.'

'Vincenzo...'

Amy tried to interrupt but her voice had no strength. Her throat seemed to have dried in the lazy, languorous heat that was licking along her veins, radiating from the point at which his hand curled around her wrist. It suffused her whole body with a warmth that made her feel as if she were bathed in the blaze of the noonday sun instead of the cool, pale light of the moon.

'Do you know how it has been for me these past four years? I have been a married man, but a married man with no wife. I put my ring on the hand of the most beautiful, most desirable woman I had ever met. I spent one night with her. One hot, passionate, sensual night—the sort of night I remember in my dreams and wake soaked in sweat—aching—*hungry*...'

'Don't...'

Amy shifted restlessly from one foot to the other and back again, her clouded gaze still locked with his, seeing the burn of memory in the depths of his eyes.

And that memory flared in her own thoughts too, playing out a series of erotic images on the screen of her mind. Images of hunger and yearning, of kisses, caresses that made her shiver just to remember them. Of the warm, bronze satin of Vincenzo's skin; the silken slide of his ebony hair under her clutching fingertips. The tangle of his muscular, hair-roughened limbs with the smooth nakedness of her own. The need that began as an ache low down in her body and then spiralled swiftly out of control, suffusing every inch of her, taking possession of her body, until she was nothing but one raw, screaming pulse of hunger...

'One night,' Vincenzo repeated, his voice cracking on the words. 'One night of ecstasy, and since then—nothing. Not a damn thing! Can you imagine how that felt?'

'Imagine? I don't have to imagine. I lived through it, too.'

Every aching, tormenting second of loss. Every moment of yearning, of hunger, of emptiness. Every sleepless night when she had lain awake, staring at the ceiling of her room with burning, dry eyes, too desolate, too broken even to find the release of tears.

But she had *loved* him and known the agony of the loss of that love. All Vincenzo was talking about was the *physical* deprivation—the sexual frustration that had eaten at him.

'Then you'll know it was not enough!'

Vincenzo's dark head lowered until his forehead rested

on the smooth silkiness of her hair, his breath softly warm against her skin.

'Never, ever enough.'

Standing like this, it was impossible to look away again. She was held transfixed by his eyes, drawn into the deep, burning pools, drowning in them.

'I cannot live on my memories for four years, Amy. And if you feel the same, then neither can you.'

It wasn't her memories that were troubling her now. It was something that was very definitely in the present. The molten burn of Vincenzo's gaze, the faint sound of his breathing, the clean, intensely personal scent of his skin. He was so close; so very, very close. She could feel the warmth of his body enclose her like the finest heated silk.

'It's been—hard...'

What *was* she saying? She didn't want him to hear this!

She had vowed to herself that she would never reveal a thing to Vincenzo. That she would never, ever let him see just how badly he had hurt her, just what she had been through since she had left him and gone home to England. And yet now it seemed that every time she opened her mouth another admission slid out that betrayed her, scraping off another protective layer of skin and leaving her even more exposed and vulnerable than before.

She must have had rather more of the delicious champagne cocktails than was wise, loosening her tongue dangerously as a result.

'What I want is right here, right now,' Vincenzo told her huskily. 'But I need to know that you feel the same.'

The smallest movement of his head was all that it took to bring his mouth into contact with hers. The soft touch of his lips was like the lick of flame over the delicate skin, setting off a searing electrical charge that pulsed along every already shockingly sensitised nerve.

'So tell me, *cara mia...*' he murmured against her mouth, his lips tracing the outline of hers in tiny, delicate kisses. 'Tell me what you want and I will give it to you. Tell me what you thought of in those long dark nights...'

His lips took hers again in another, more demanding kiss, one that opened her mouth, let his tongue slide intimately over the delicate surfaces exposed to it. Strong hands were in her hair, tangling in the silken strands, drawing her head back so that he could deepen the caress.

It wasn't the champagne that had intoxicated her—nothing so simple. Instead it was Vincenzo himself and the lean strength of his body, the heady mixture of the scent of his skin and the tang of bergamot in his aftershave. The husky enticement of his words that went straight to her heart with a force more potent than any of the most unadulterated spirit.

'Cenzo...'

The name escaped her on a soft moan, feeling alien on her tongue. The long-ago, almost forgotten, intimately familiar, affectionate shortening of his name that he would only allow his immediate family to use. His immediate family—and his wife.

'Si, carissima.'

It was the softest of whispers and he moved closer as he spoke, crushing her up against the pillar of the street lamp, the metal cold and hard at her back.

But the front of her body was all warmth, all fire, and another, very different form of hardness, heated velvet and steel, was pressed into the cradle of her hips, communicating in the most basic, most primitively eloquent way the potent force of his physical need for her. The stinging points of her breasts were up against the hard wall of his chest, the strength of his legs imprisoned her slender limbs as yet another of those sensually, drugging kisses drained the strength from her body.

Without the support of the lamp at her back, she was sure she would collapse, sinking to the ground in a mindless heap. And her thoughts too seemed to have blown a fuse, incapable of being forced into any sort of coherent order.

'I know how you feel...' Vincenzo whispered in her ear, strong white teeth softly nibbling at the delicate outer edge so that she writhed against him in instinctive response. 'Your body speaks to me eloquently, so you don't have to say a word. But I want you body and soul, so you must tell me. You must say what you want, tell me everything...'

'Cenzo...'

Amy had no idea at all what she was going to say, whether to accede or to deny him. But even as she spoke, out on the canal a crowded *vaporetto* moved past in a blur of light and sound, a faint ripple of applause and laughter reaching to them across the water.

Immediately his long body froze, his proud head coming up slightly. With his cheek still against hers, the sudden tension in his strong jaw communicating his abrupt change of mood, Vincenzo cursed softly in Italian.

'*Per Dio*, this is not the time or the place.'

After the scorching intensity of his passionate undertones just moments earlier, the thread of laughter in his voice was shocking, unbelievable.

'Amy, *bellissima mia*, we must continue this elsewhere. Somewhere more suitable for what I have in mind.'

With his hands on the lamp-post, he levered himself backwards away from her, the darkly mesmeric power of his eyes still holding her captive as forcefully as his physical strength had done just moments before. Without the warm power of his body between her and the night, the rush of cold air over her hotly sensitised flesh was a burning shock that made Amy cry out in agitation and distress.

'Hush, *cara*, hush,' he soothed, the shake in his voice a disturbing blend of understanding, amusement, and dangerous triumph. 'I know how you feel, but this is not the end—it is a beginning.'

With a gesture that had an old-worldly courtliness that

matched their surroundings perfectly, he held out his hand to her, watching, waiting—willing her, she was convinced, to put her own into it.

'Come home with me. Come back to my house and let me show you how it can be, now that you are here with me at last. Let me make you forget those long, cold nights, teach you how it should have been, how it could be again...'

It was impossible to think; impossible to question. She could only react, following the most primal instincts that had possession of all her senses. And those instincts pushed her to lift a shaking hand, to lace her trembling fingers with Vincenzo's firm, sure ones, and feel their strength close about her.

And when he moved she could only follow, stumbling after him on high, delicate heels. It was either that or fall flat on her face, because without his strength to support her she couldn't move or function. She even feared she might actually have to force herself to breathe, so complete was her abandonment of herself to his control.

What remained of their journey was completed in silence; only Vincenzo's hurried stride, so swift and long that Amy had to trot inelegantly in order to keep up with it, betrayed anything about his mental state, the urgency of feeling that had him in its grip. But when they reached the house they had barely set foot inside, the door still closing behind them, before he swung her back into his arms and took her mouth with a searing sexual impatience.

'I swore I would wait,' he muttered against her mouth. 'I promised—but I cannot keep that promise any longer. Amy—'

Once more, what he had been about to say was choked off as he plundered her lips with a ferocity that made her head swim, and Amy found she was kissing him back, offering touch for touch, caress for caress.

Her hands tugged the silk tie loose at his throat, wrenching the buttons beneath it open with fingers made clumsy with need. In the same moment, the velvet evening coat was pushed from her shoulders, the heat of Vincenzo's mouth burning the exposed skin as he trailed kisses towards the base of her throat where a wild pulse throbbed desperately.

'Cenzo!' His name was a sound of longing, a litany of need on her lips. 'Cenzo...Cenzo...'

She broke off on a shaken cry of delight as she felt the heated hardness of his palms against her breasts, cupping their soft weight through the rich velvet of her dress. Pleasure burned an aching path of need down the length of her body, to centre in a molten pool deep inside at the juncture of her thighs. She couldn't hold back a low, keening sound of response as she writhed against him, pressing herself close against the swollen evidence of his forceful arousal.

'Per Dio!' Vincenzo choked, the words rough and hard at the base of his throat.

Abruptly she was released again, his dark head shaking from side to side in amazement at his own reaction.

'Look what you do to me,' he muttered thickly. 'You make me forget who I am, where I am.'

With a half rueful, half disbelieving smile, he looked down into her navy eyes, seeing the desire and hunger that burned there, mirroring his own.

'Upstairs?' he questioned roughly and Amy needed no elaboration or explanation as to what the single, husky word might mean.

'Upstairs...'

She was frankly surprised that her voice worked. Everything else in her body seemed to have shut down, ceasing to function, so that she couldn't move away from the spot where he had left her, couldn't focus on anything but him. Without his arms around her, his touch on her skin, she felt lost, bereft in a way that was like a scream of pain in her soul. The blazing arousal that his kisses and caresses had awoken still had her in its power, refusing to recede so that she trembled in the force of its grip.

'I'm taking you upstairs,' Vincenzo said on a very different note, one that was all urgency and impatience, the aching need inside making the word crack in the middle. 'No argument.'

The words had barely left his tongue before she was gathered into his arms, lifted off her feet and carried up the stairs; Vincenzo found his way with a sure-footed confidence that was belied by the way his gaze was still locked with hers, his eyes never leaving her face for a second.

On the landing, her door was the first they came to, and he kicked it open with a force and lack of ceremony that betrayed only too clearly the ferocity of the passion that had him in its grip. The velvet evening coat had slid off and been discarded somewhere along their route, her fine leather shoes falling to the floor with a thud as he crossed the room to be booted away with supreme indifference to where they finally ended up.

His hands were already reaching for the zip at the back of her dress, even as he deposited her on the soft blue quilt with such force that the breath escaped from her lungs in a muffled gasp.

'This has to go,' he muttered harshly, his breathing raw and uneven, a wild flash of colour marking the wide, slanting cheekbones. 'I want to see you...really see you. I want you naked...'

It was what she wanted too, and she wriggled energetically on the bed, helping him pull the tight-fitting dress from her body. In the struggle she heard something tear savagely but she was beyond feeling even a pang of regret for the expensive garment, able only to feel thankful that she was now free of its constricting folds. As he tossed aside the crumpled velvet, Vincenzo's breath hissed in through his teeth as his dark eyes surveyed her slender body lying pillowed on the downy quilt, the tiny scraps of lace at her breasts and hips, and the finest of black stockings her only covering.

'*Dio!*'

The sound was wrenched from him with shocking force and she saw the way his throat worked as he swallowed hard.

'You are even more beautiful than I remember...'

Kneeling on the bed, he leaned back, burning eyes searing over every exposed inch, his hooded gaze heavy with sensual appreciation.

'More beautiful than in my dreams, and there you were a fantasy come true. No!'

He moved swiftly to stop her as, in a sudden agony of embarrassment at being exposed like this, being the subject of such a deliberate, calculated scrutiny, Amy tried to fold her arms across the creamy swell of breasts pushed provocatively up and together by the smoky grey lace and lycra of her bra.

'*No!*' he repeated more emphatically, his accent growing thicker than she had ever heard it on the single word as he caught and imprisoned her hands.

Hard fingers closed around both wrists, forcing them up above her head and holding them down on the pillows, the beautiful shape of his mouth curving into a smile of darkly sensual delight.

'Never cover yourself up in front of me, Amy, *innamorata*,' he commanded harshly. 'Never try to hide the beauty of your body from my eyes. I am your husband, and as your husband I have the right to see every glorious inch of you...'

His eyes blazed with burning satisfaction.

'To do more than see...'

Slowly he reached out with his free hand and trailed tantalising fingertips across the smooth skin of her forehead, down past her eye, along the soft curve of her cheek.

'I can touch you here…and here…'

That tormenting hand moved lower, caressed her shoulder, taking with it the delicate strap of her bra, sliding it down her arm until the lace that curved around her breast loosened, slipped, exposing the hard, tight bud of her nipple.

'And here…'

'Vincenzo!' Amy gasped, writhing in the grip of a pleasure so sharp it was dangerously close to pain as a long, tanned index finger moved to circle the responsive peak, his touch sending shockwaves of rapture reverberating along every nerve.

'Do you like that, sweetheart?' His voice was a tiger's purr, rich with triumph. 'Well there's more where that came from. How about if I touch you here?'

This time it was the flat palm of his hand, hot and hard, that slithered fully into the cup of the bra, lifting her breast with its pouting nipple to meet the warm moist caress of his mouth. Amy could only fling back her head and moan aloud as his tongue traced the same erotic path that his fingertip had followed just seconds before, his teeth delicately grazing the tender skin, rousing a stinging pleasure that threatened to shatter her self control completely.

'*Buono,*' Vincenzo murmured, lifting his dark head, and looking straight into her flushed face. 'And this?'

'This' was to take the whole tip of her breast into the heat of his mouth, suckling softly until she arched her back, mutely inviting a fiercer, more passionate caress. The warm breath of Vincenzo's laughter feathered across her sensitised skin, sending shivers of response down her spine.

'You like that, *cara*?' he questioned, when she was unable to hold back the incoherent murmurs of protest at the way he had taken his mouth away, depriving her of the pleasure that had gripped her. 'Is that what you dreamed of in those long lonely nights? Was that where you longed for my touch? Or perhaps it was here…'

Once more his teasing fingers moved over her skin, tracing hot erotic patterns across the tops of her breasts, flushed now with the heated blood that had risen to the surface in response to her hectic breathing. Weakly, impotently, Amy fought against his restraining grip, only to freeze again as she registered the track his hand was taking, its path unmistakable, its ultimate destination painfully clear.

Her breath caught in her throat as she stilled, waiting, unable to move. His dark eyes locking with hers, Vincenzo watched every flicker of response, every tiny, uncontrollable reaction in her face as his caresses moved lower.

A second later he deliberately slid his hand up and away from the burning centre of her femininity, bringing a choking cry of protest from her lips. His expression intent, he paused, changed direction yet again, let it drift down, then up...

Then, just as she was reduced to digging her teeth into the fullness of her lower lip in order to hold back the frantic cry of agonised frustration, he suddenly moved with firm decisiveness, sliding under the smoke-coloured silk to curve the strength of his hand over the damp heat of the most feminine core of her body.

'So this is what you wanted,' he muttered, acting the part of surprised discovery to perfection. 'Well, why didn't you say? You only had to ask...'

'Vincenzo!'

Amy's head tossed from side to side on the pillows. It was impossible to hide the way she was feeling, the devastating effect he was having on her. She was lost, adrift on the wildest sea of passion she had ever experienced, totally under Vincenzo's control, and the worst part was that she didn't even give a damn about the way that made her look.

Vincenzo's smile was darkly triumphant as he bent his head to take her lips once more. The kiss swamped her with sensation so that she closed her eyes tight shut in a

vain attempt to control them. So it was in total darkness
that she heard his voice, and the cruel satisfaction in it as
he spoke again.

'I knew you were mine from the start. Mine and mine
alone. I knew that once I touched you, once I had you, you
could never go with anyone else. Never think of anyone
else; never respond to anyone else. You are mine...'

*Mine and mine alone. This time, when I take you, I will
hold you for ever. I will never let you go again.*

Sex and possession. The power over her that Vincenzo
wanted so much he could not believe that she could look
at any other man.

She had fallen completely into that power once and it
had almost destroyed her. How could she be so blind, so
foolish as to risk letting it happen all over again?

'No!'

If he had flung a bucket of ice cold water right in her
face he couldn't have extinguished the blazing hunger his
kisses and caresses had awoken any more effectively.

'I said *no!*'

With a strength she hadn't known she had possessed,
Amy wrenched her mouth away from Vincenzo's kisses,
her arms away from the grip that imprisoned them above
her head. The force of the movement threw her away and
to her right, coming to the edge of the wide bed before she
had time to think it might be there so that she tumbled
inelegantly from the high, firm mattress. With a small cry
of shock she landed painfully on the floor where the thick
pile of the carpet only barely cushioned her fall.

'What the devil...?'

Vincenzo's response was positively the last straw. Where
she had expected shock, probably anger, possibly even
hard, bitterly frustrated disbelief, the sardonic amusement
that lit his dark eyes from within was much more than she
could bear.

'Amy, *mia cara*, just what are you doing now? I know

you are the most passionately responsive female it has ever been my pleasure to bed, but surely...'

'This,' Amy declared through gritted teeth, getting to her feet with as much of the shattered remnants of dignity as she was able to gather round her, 'has nothing to do with response or passion, and it very definitely has no connection at all with your *pleasure*!'

'On the contrary, it has everything to do with it,' Vincenzo drawled with sardonic humour. 'Or, rather, everything to do with a major discomfort I'm currently feeling—but that's something you can put right just as soon as you stop behaving like an outraged virginal nun who's just woken up to find the local Don Juan in her bed.'

'I'm not doing any such thing! I may actually be the biggest fool in the world for letting this happen, but believe me, I'm not *acting*—very far from it!'

'Amy, *innamorata*, you're not making any sort of sense. Would you mind explaining...'

'This isn't going to happen!' Amy interjected furiously, unable to take any more of his coldly mocking tone. 'It mustn't! It's wrong!'

'Wrong?'

She'd surprised him there. He really couldn't quite believe what he'd heard.

'*Sbaglio*? How can it be wrong?'

He raked one strong brown hand roughly through his hair in bemusement at her declaration and the furious tone in which she had flung it at him.

'I am your husband. You are my wife. That means that this is not *wrong*. On the contrary, it's completely, utterly *right*. It's *right* that we should lust after each other; *right* that I should want to kiss you, touch you, make love to you.'

'*Love?*' Amy echoed on a snort of contempt that matched his perfectly. 'It—'

'And it's right that you should go to pieces when I do

these things,' Vincenzo inserted smoothly, taking the rug right from under her feet. 'That you can't wait to let me take you to bed and make mad, passionate love all night long.'

'Only if we love one another!'

That stopped him dead. His dark head went back sharply, jet-black eyes narrowing until they were merely gleaming slits under hooded lids and thick black lashes.

'You don't?' he questioned sharply.

'Love you?'

Reaction was setting in fast; Amy was trembling all over, struggling to get her wildly seesawing emotions back under control. And her aroused body was beginning to protest furiously at the abrupt ending to the glorious lovemaking it had been experiencing, the removal of the powerful sexual climax every awakened nerve had been anticipating eagerly.

'No, I don't love you. You killed any love I had for you by the way you treated me.'

Had that hit home? His face gave nothing away, but there was a long, nerve-stretching pause before Vincenzo shrugged in supreme indifference.

'No matter. We don't need love for what we have between us.'

'Vincenzo, no!'

Amy jumped backwards as he made a move to come towards her, his purpose written clearly on those stunning features.

'You may not need love, but *I do*! And—and...'

She struggled desperately for inspiration, grabbing at it thankfully when a germ of an idea presented itself. The only thing that might possibly make Vincenzo hold back.

'I—I've found it with someone else.'

'Someone else?'

It was obvious he couldn't believe it, that she had rocked his male pride so severely that he was unable to believe that she would even dare to look at anyone else, let alone actually put them in his place.

'What exactly are you saying?'

As always in times of stress or anger, his accent had deepened, becoming much more pronounced. And the look of dark fury in his eyes threatened to shrivel every word on her tongue.

'Amy?' It was ominous, dangerous, laced with warning. Amy swallowed hard; forced herself to speak.

'I've met someone else,' she improvised wildly. 'That's why I'm here. I came to tell you—I want to marry him.'

CHAPTER SIX

IT WAS worse than she had ever thought it might be.

She had anticipated anger. Perhaps fierce, black fury, or the sort of freezing withdrawal that was a Vincenzo Ravenelli speciality. Or possibly a refusal to listen, to believe a word she had to say.

She got none of that. Instead she was treated to a withering scorn; to the sort of mocking cynicism that seemed to wrench her soul right out of her breast.

'You want to *marry* him?' Vincenzo repeated on a note of such disdain that she winced inwardly just to hear it. 'Is that a fact? Tell me, my dear wife, do they really do things so very differently in England?'

'D-differently?'

Vincenzo's smile was pure acid, eating away at her heart with its travesty of kindliness and understanding for the simple-minded.

'I realise that it may be not quite what you're used to, but here in Italy it is usual to get rid of one bridegroom before you acquire another. I believe that the name for marrying two at once—'

'I know very well what the name for that is!' Amy snapped furiously. 'And of course I know that I can't marry two men at once. Obviously, that's precisely why I'm here. But I really can't carry on this sort of a conversation under these circumstances!'

'And what circumstances are those?'

'Isn't it obvious?' She gestured wildly to where he stood, one dark eyebrow raised in enquiry. 'You are fully clothed...'

Except for the tie she had wrenched away, the buttons

74

her clutching fingers had pulled open, exposing a disturbing amount of smoothly muscled, olive-skinned chest, the shadows of black curling hair arrowing down to the narrow leather belt that encircled his slim waist...

No!

With a shudder of reaction she dragged her weak thoughts away from the wanton path they were taking, forcing herself not to look anywhere but into Vincenzo's face. Immediately she wished she hadn't as she felt the full icy force of his baleful glare, bitter as a freezing wind from the North.

'While I—I'm not suitably dressed at all!'

'On the contrary. You are perfectly dressed for what I have in mind.'

'And we both know what that is!'

'It seems to me that it was exactly what was on your mind too until a moment or so ago,' Vincenzo retorted smoothly.

He was obviously not a prey to her own fears about looking anywhere but into her face as he let his smouldering black gaze move over her from top to toe in a blatantly sexual survey.

'And, really, I am thoroughly enjoying the view.'

'Well, the view is all you're going to get!'

Spotting her navy cotton dressing gown draped over a nearby chair, Amy pounced on it thankfully, pulling the garment on with such haste that when she fastened the belt the whole thing was distinctly lop-sided. Not that she gave a damn about that, she told herself, tying a second secure bow for good measure. As long as she was covered from neck to toe she felt better, her chin lifting higher as some degree of composure and courage returned.

'Better?' Vincenzo enquired with the sort of false concern that had Amy's teeth snapping together as she bit back the very rude, very angry retort that she was tempted to express. 'Are you ready to talk now?'

She would have preferred to suggest that they move elsewhere. The combination of Vincenzo's tall, powerfully male frame, those frankly lascivious eyes, and the softly padded king-size bed—a bed on which only moments before she had been writhing in the closest thing to erotic ecstasy this side of an orgasm—was not at all conducive to clear thought and logical argument.

But to declare as much was to admit a weakness that she was painfully sure that Vincenzo would pounce on immediately, giving her no quarter. And so she managed to nod her head, smoothing down the navy robe until she realised that the way her hands shook betrayed her more than anything she could say.

'As ready as I'll ever be—not that there's much to talk about.'

She considered sitting on the edge of the bed, then rethought hastily as she recalled just why the blue and cream coverlet was especially crumpled in that particular spot. Instead she moved to the nearest chair, holding onto its back for support as she faced him once more.

'It's perfectly simple, Vincenzo. I've met someone else.'

She was amazed at the ease with which the lies formed on her tongue.

'He hasn't asked me to marry him, yet, but I know that's what's on his mind. And obviously I can't say yes until I— I'm free from our marriage. That's why I came here. To tell you that I want a divorce.'

There, it was done! She said it at last, and in the end it hadn't been quite as dreadful as she had feared. Once she had got started, the words had come pouring out, tangling on her tongue, almost tripping over themselves in her haste to have them finally spoken. And it hadn't been completely untrue; just a touch of embroidery on reality. The end result was the same. She wanted a divorce. But not because she planned to marry anyone else.

But as the seconds ticked by and Vincenzo still hadn't

reacted or answered she was forced to doubt her own sanity, wondering whether in fact she had actually spoken the words aloud and not just framed them inside her head.

'Vincenzo?' she managed uncertainly. 'Did you hear…?'

'Hear? Of course I heard.'

'Then what…?'

'You want a response?' he questioned when her voice failed her as her apprehensive blue gaze met the unyielding force of his black one. 'Why?'

'I—I would have thought that was obvious. I need an answer.'

'And I would have thought that *that* was obvious,' Vincenzo tossed back, his tone totally devoid of emotion. 'Why ask for an answer when you know already what it will be? But if you want me to spell it out…'

She didn't want anything spelling out. She could already guess what was coming and her heart quailed inside simply at anticipating it. But she didn't even dare to try to stop Vincenzo now.

'You want to know if I'll give you a divorce? The answer is no—never! The Ravenelli family do not divorce.'

Well, she'd asked for it! Whatever else, she'd hoped that at least he would go as far as to consider the idea, not just dismiss it out of hand. Only the thought of the new start she had dreamed of, if she could win her freedom, spurred her on to argue with him.

'They must…'

The shake of his head was a total rejection of her protest.

'No way. No member of my family has ever undergone the ignominy of the divorce courts, and I have no intention of being the first one.'

'Well, tough!' Despair made Amy assume a hardness she was very far from feeling. 'I want this and one way or another I'm going to get it! I can always divorce you without your consent!'

'You can send me any papers you like. I will never sign them.'

'But you *must*!'

No, telling Vincenzo Ravenelli that he *must* do anything was the worst possible idea. From the flare of cold anger in his eyes, the new tension in his strong jawline, she knew that all she was doing was hardening his resolve. She was just making him even more determined to thwart her desire, if it was at all possible.

'Vincenzo, please!'

Was the man made of stone? How could he look at her like that? How could he look into her pleading eyes, see the glisten of the tears she couldn't quite control, and still show no flicker of concern?

But wasn't this just what she should have expected? Wasn't this the man who had married her simply in order to get her into his bed, and to win a lousy, stinking *bet*?

'You have to give me a divorce—or, at the very least, you can't stop me! We've been separated for four years— in another twelve months I can divorce you with or without your consent. When I tell a judge how you conned me into marrying you, how you deceived me, it'll be obvious straight away that you never meant ours to be a real marriage at all! That the whole thing was a lie from start to finish.'

'And when I tell him how you've behaved since you arrived in Italy, it'll be even more obvious that you don't know your own mind—that you're not really certain whether you want this marriage to end or not,' Vincenzo shot back, with the air of a medieval knight throwing down a gauntlet in arrogant challenge.

'That I...?'

Where had that come from? She'd had no warning of the way his thoughts were heading and he had attacked with the speed and venom of a striking snake.

'What are you talking about?'

'About you, my beloved wife, and the mixed messages you've been giving me ever since you arrived in Italy—the way you've been blowing hot and cold, giving me the come-on one moment—'

'Giving you the...?' Amy could only shake her head in disbelieving confusion 'I did no such thing! You set out from the first to seduce *me*! I—I...'

'Look at it from my point of view, *cara*. When my wife turns up on my doorstep, what am I to think? I truly believed that you had come to your senses. That you had come to build bridges, to try to start again with our marriage—and, obviously, I thought that that included a return to a physical relationship.'

'Obviously,' Amy echoed hollowly, sinking down into the chair she had been leaning against, her legs refusing to support her without trembling.

'Especially when you behaved as if it was what you wanted most in all the world.'

Amy's head came up in protest, blue eyes flashing rejection of his outrageous assertion.

'Now, that is just not true!'

'No?' Vincenzo queried, black eyes rounding in a look of fake astonishment that gave her a rush of new strength, pushing her out of the chair and halfway across the room towards him. 'Look at it from my point of view.'

'I don't want to look at anything from your warped, twisted point of view!'

Having come this far across the room, Amy didn't quite know what to do with herself and came to an awkward, stumbling halt to stand, her hands clenched into fists at her sides, glaring at him furiously.

'I wouldn't trust you not to distort everything so that it fitted your perverted version of the truth instead of what actually happened.'

'Perverted,' Vincenzo echoed, his intonation sending ice sliding down her spine, making her quail inwardly at the danger threatened by his coolly precise enunciation. 'Distorted. Let me see...'

He swung away from her, prowling slowly around the room, looking for all the world like a big, sleek black panther restlessly pacing the confines of its cage. He gave the impression of having to think of what he wanted to say, but Amy suspected that it was nothing but show. She had never seen Vincenzo at a loss for words in any way, and she certainly didn't expect him to start now.

Pivoting on his heel, Vincenzo turned back to her, one hand held up, one long finger extended to emphasise his point.

'You come to my house with little warning—just a telephone message left to say you're arriving. What am I to think?'

'You've already told me what you thought!' Amy managed through gritted teeth. 'And *I* have told you that you were mistaken.'

'So you have.' With a lift of his broad shoulders he shrugged off her interjection. 'But was I mistaken about the fact that you made no mention at all of any thought of divorce?'

A second tanned finger joined the first to count off another argument.

'Or that you agreed to act as my wife in public and in private?'

'I...'

Amy buried her face in her hands as the memory of her own foolish behaviour came back to haunt her. She hadn't had the courage to be straight with him from the start and as a result she had fallen headfirst into a deep, dangerous trap that she hadn't even seen yawning beneath her until now, when it was far, far too late.

'You agreed to stay in my home. You wore the clothes I bought for you,' Vincenzo continued relentlessly, bombarding her with evidence like the counsel for the prosecution until she felt physically bruised and battered by his attacking tone. 'And not just the clothes—the jewellery.'

His voice dropped an octave, became a deep, husky whisper.

'You still wear it now.'

Defensively Amy's fingers flew to her neck, clutching at the diamond necklace she had forgotten was around her throat. Silently she cursed the moment of weak vanity that had driven her to putting it on in the first place.

'You even made it plain that you wanted what was due to you—the four extra stones,' Vincenzo explained harshly when she frowned her confusion at his meaning. 'For the years of our so-called marriage.'

'Exactly!' Amy jumped on the let-out clause she thought he had given her. 'Our *so-called* marriage! What is there to make you think..?'

'You kissed me.' Vincenzo dismissed her interjection with a contemptuous flick of his hand. 'More than that… ''Cenzo!…Cenzo!'''

To her horror he mimicked her own reaction earlier with near-perfect accuracy, capturing the breathless tone, the hungry urgency, in a way that had the hot blood flooding into her face, burning her skin.

'Stop it! Stop it, you monster!' She stamped her foot hard to emphasise her words. 'I don't want to hear this!'

'I don't give a damn what you want or don't want!' Vincenzo tossed at her, his sudden complete stillness, the taut, antagonistic stance of his tall, lean body somehow even more disturbing than the restless, predatory prowling of just moments before. 'I'm telling you what happened. How it seemed to me—and how it will seem to any judge who hears my side of the story. And we haven't covered everything yet.'

'Oh, I'll bet we haven't!' Amy muttered cynically, twisting the narrow belt of her robe round and round in her hands until it had formed into wild, tangled knots. 'So what else it there? What other nasty little stories do you have to tell?'

'Nothing but the truth about the way you melted into my arms. The way you went up in flames when I kissed you; turned into a wildcat when I touched you. The way you came with me here—came willingly—more than willingly to your bedroom—to that bed.'

Reluctantly Amy's shadowed eyes went to the duvet on the bed, seeing again the creases in the blue cotton cover, the unmistakable evidence of the passion that had gripped her such a short time before. A passion that was now so dead and cold that she couldn't recall ever having experienced it. A passion that made her sick to her stomach even to contemplate.

'Nothing happened,' she muttered ungraciously, stubbornly keeping her head averted, avoiding his eyes, unable to face the look of cynical contempt she knew must be in them.

'Nothing?' Vincenzo echoed mockingly. '*Niente*? I wonder would a judge see it that way? Correct me if I'm wrong, but doesn't sleeping with your estranged husband negate any separation there has been, meaning you have to start all over again?'

'We didn't *sleep together*!' Amy protested furiously. 'I told you—nothing happened! We…'

'And what about your prospective fiancé?' Vincenzo cut across her outburst as if it had never been, blithely ignoring the way she had swung round to face him again, the black glare she turned on him. 'What would he think if he knew that when you were here, supposedly asking for a divorce, for your freedom so that you could marry him, you actually fell into my arms?'

'I did not!'

'Kissed me like I was the only man in the world?'

'No-o!'

'Enticed me, seduced me. Came on to me in a way that

no man with red blood in his veins could resist. What would he think if he knew that tonight, when he thought you were safe and sound in your modest, innocent, single bed, in fact you were all over me for all you could get?'

'*No!*'

Driven beyond endurance, Amy launched at him, hand held high, palm flattened, ready to slap the cold contempt from his eyes, the callous sneer from his beautiful mouth. She didn't care that she had led him into this. That by inventing her own story of a fictitious fiancé she had given him the ammunition he needed; she only wanted to silence his hateful taunts.

But fast as she moved, Vincenzo's reactions were quicker. Acting on instincts that went deeper than thought, his own hand came up, catching her wrist and holding it still, suspended in the air just inches away from his face.

'What is it, sweetheart?' he murmured, holding her furious blue gaze with his own hypnotic dark eyed stare. 'Don't you like the truth?'

'Those disgusting thoughts couldn't be further from the truth if they tried!'

The way one black brow lifted, questioning her assertion, only incensed her further, making her fight to free herself from his imprisoning hold, only conceding defeat when it became obvious that her struggles were worse than useless against his strength.

'So you're claiming that your behaviour had nothing to do with the discovery that I now own all of Ravenelli Enterprises? That I'm now a much wealthier man than you ever dreamed possible?'

'I'm claiming nothing!'

With an effort Amy forced herself to meet his cold-eyed glare head on. She couldn't weaken now or he would move in for the kill, pouncing on her as a tiger jumps on its weakened prey.

'I'm not giving your foul suggestion the distinction of

considering it, never mind bothering with an answer. It's not worth it!'

'And your would-be fiancé? What's his name?'

What's his name? David's was the only one that came to mind and she didn't hesitate. The two men would never come up against each other anyway.

'It's David—David Brooke—but he wouldn't worry about anything like that. He wouldn't even ask.'

'He must have great faith in you,' Vincenzo drawled cynically. 'Either that or he's a blind, besotted fool. I wonder which one it is.'

'Wouldn't you like to know?' Amy flung the words into his shuttered, watchful face, her chin lifting defiantly. 'What a pity you'll have no way of finding out because if I have my way you'll never, ever meet him.'

The words were barely out of her mouth when a sound from across the room brought her head whipping round to stare in disbelieving horror in the direction of her handbag, discarded on the floor in the heat of the passion that had gripped her such a short time before.

Earlier that evening, she had tried to phone David again, this time at home, but had only managed to connect with his answering machine. After leaving a message she had fully intended to switch off her mobile again, but had obviously forgotten to do so. And now, with the worst sort of timing possible, David was ringing her.

CHAPTER SEVEN

'Aren't you going to answer it?'

'What?'

Amy turned slowly back to Vincenzo, struggling to focus her dazed, shocked eyes on his still, watchful face.

'The phone,' he repeated with a touch of irritation. 'Aren't you going to answer it?'

'Oh—no. It'll be nothing important.'

She had thought she'd sounded convincing, indifferent enough to distract his attention. But some unwary movement, some flicker of a response she couldn't hide at the thought of Vincenzo confronting David about their supposed relationship had given her away, alerting his suspicions at once.

'It's him!' he declared sharply. '*Il fidanzato*—the so-special David!'

'No...' Amy began protestingly. 'No, you're wrong. It wouldn't be...'

But she was speaking to empty air. Before she had time to register he had moved, to realise his intent, Vincenzo had released his grip on her wrist, dropping her hand unceremoniously, and was already on the other side of the room, snatching up her handbag.

'No!'

Heedless of the way that her belated reaction revealed her earlier response for the lie it was, Amy launched herself across the blue carpet after him, her hand outstretched to grab the bag from him.

She was too late. Finding her mobile by the simple expedient of upending the bag over the bed so that all its

85

contents tumbled out on to the quilt, Vincenzo snatched up the phone and thumbed the button that switched it on.

'*Si?*' he barked into the receiver.

The momentary silence, a look on Vincenzo's listening face, told its own story. Amy could just imagine David's stunned reaction, hear his shocked, '*Who* is that?' and the thought was enough to bring her up sharp, pausing momentarily in her headlong rush. And that in its turn was long enough to give Vincenzo time to add to the problem, stirring things deliberately.

'My name is Vincenzo Ravenelli,' he drawled, forcing Amy to wonder whether the cynical amusement in his voice was as obvious to David far away in England as it was to her here in this room. 'Yes, she's here…'

The swift glance he slanted in Amy's direction, the wicked glint of a cruel amusement in his dark eyes broke through the shock that held Amy frozen, sparking off a hot anger that had her lurching forward again.

'How dare you? You have no right—that's mine!'

She tried to snatch the phone from him, only to be thwarted by a swift side-step, a half turn to the right so that her hand landed impotently on his shoulder instead of on the mobile.

'Would you like to speak to her?' Vincenzo continued imperturbably, addressing the other man with an easy warmth that made it seem as if they were long-term friends. Amy's blood pressure shot skywards just imagining what David must be thinking, how he would be taking this. 'Just a moment…'

Turning round again, he held the phone out to Amy with a smile that set her teeth on edge.

'He wants to talk to you. It's David…'

'I know damn well who… Oh, hi, David!'

Amy adjusted her tone hastily, bringing the volume down as she moved towards the window, as far from Vincenzo as possible. She was painfully aware of the fact that David would pick up any hint of her mood, and the last thing she wanted was for him to realise just how uptight she was.

But David wouldn't have noticed. He was too intrigued by the reception his call had received.

'Just who the hell was that?' he demanded as soon as he heard Amy's voice.

'He's—his name's Vincenzo Ravenelli...'

Silently Amy cursed the sudden attack of nerves that put the unwanted shake into her voice. She knew the impression it would give to the dark, silently watchful man on the other side of the room. She turned to look at Vincenzo again, switching on an icy glare.

'This is a private conversation,' she hissed. 'Do you mind?'

She should have known there was no point in trying to appeal to his better nature, mainly because he didn't have one. He didn't try to disguise the fact that he was listening to every word, settling himself on the bed, and lounging back against the pillows with every appearance of enjoyment. He even switched on a wide, brilliant smile. One that Amy determinedly ignored—it was either that or throw something at him—as she turned her attention back to the phone.

'I know what his name is.' David's voice was tart. 'He told me that. But who is he?'

'He...'

In spite of herself, Amy couldn't suppress the swift sidelong glance that slid in Vincenzo's direction. When she met the full force of his cold-eyed, expressionless stare, her heart skipped a beat painfully, and she dropped her gaze again as she struggled to find an answer.

'He's—just someone I met.'

Out of the corner of her eye she caught the slight movement as Vincenzo's dark head lifted, watchful and attentive. She could just imagine what his quick, incisive brain would make of *that*; the sort of thoughts that must be clicking over inside his head, considering, assessing…

'*Ravenelli.*' Realisation had struck David. 'Do you mean *the* Vincenzo Ravenelli?'

'Mmm. That's right.'

'You're moving in some pretty exalted circles!' David was obviously impressed. 'That guy is seriously loaded.'

'I'm sure…'

It suddenly occurred to Amy that she was playing this all wrong. She had let Vincenzo wrong-foot her from the start by answering the phone himself. Now she badly needed to regain some of the ground she had lost—and fast.

'It's good to hear from you.'

She suddenly changed her tone, putting a new enthusiasm, a breathless excitement into it.

It was a good job that Vincenzo couldn't hear the other man from where he was sitting. David was clearly taken aback by this unexpected declaration.

'Well—I just wanted you to know the good news. We got the Randerson contract.'

'Oh, David, that's brilliant!'

'Yes, it's something of a triumph. But there'll be a lot of paperwork and this temp just isn't up to your standards. So I was wondering when you're coming home.'

'I…'

When would she be able to go home? She had been so sure that this would be easy to deal with but things had turned out so very differently from the way she had expected.

A swift glance at Vincenzo warned her that her hesitation, her obvious uncertainty, had drawn his attention. She didn't want it to make him suspicious of the truth.

'I'll be home just as soon as possible. I'll give you a ring when I know my flight details.'

'I suppose that will have to do.' David was clearly none too pleased. 'I'll see you.'

With the connection safely severed, Amy decided a little extra improvisation was called for.

'Goodnight, darling,' she murmured huskily. 'Sleep well.'

For extra measure, she blew several long kisses into the receiver. She even considered trying an affecting little sigh of regret as she switched off her phone, but decided that would be taking things just too far.

And she was thankful that she hadn't bothered as she heard Vincenzo stir behind her, stretching luxuriously and linking his hands behind his head.

'He knows nothing about me, does he?'

The mobile phone dropped from Amy's hand to land with a thud on the carpet. Face white, she turned slowly to face him, feeling as if the floor was not quite steady under her feet, a disturbing buzzing noise in her ears.

'Wh-what do you mean?' she bluffed, terrified he had seen straight to the heart of her subterfuge, revealing it as the pretence it was.

Vincenzo's hard mouth curled into a cruel little smile.

'Your precious David. The so-special Mr Brooke. He was stunned—shocked when I answered the phone...'

'Of course he was! He was expecting me...' Her voice faded before the slow, adamant shake of Vincenzo's dark head.

'It was more that that. The last thing he anticipated was speaking to another man, and most definitely not an Italian. And he'd never heard my name before. Which he should have done if you'd ever mentioned it to him.'

'I don't like to talk about our marriage,' Amy protested. 'I made a mistake...'

'It's not that you don't like to talk about our marriage,' Vincenzo inserted smoothly. 'The truth is that you never have. If you had, then at least this man who you claim wants to marry you would have known my name. And you wouldn't have had to lie to him.'

'I...'

'"Just someone I met",' Vincenzo tossed at her, shooting down in flames her attempt to dodge the issue. 'So tell me, *innamorata*, does this poor fool who thinks you're here on a pleasure trip even have any idea that you already have a husband?'

Amy didn't honour that question with a reply. What was the point? He knew the answer already.

'I see!'

It was a sigh of satisfaction.

'I almost feel sorry for the sucker. He's obviously totally deceived by you. You have him dangling on a string, whispering lying sweet nothings over the phone to keep him quiet...'

'He's my fiancé!'

But her panicky vehemence was a mistake. Vincenzo's mood changed abruptly, his face hardening as he swung upright, all the indolent amusement fading from his eyes.

'Correction, *cara*,' he snapped. 'He is nothing to you while you are still my wife. And you *are* still my wife.'

'Not from choice! You can't hold me to our marriage if I want to be free! You have to let me go, Vincenzo... *Vincenzo*!'

But Vincenzo wasn't listening. He had suddenly developed an unexpected and concentrated interest in the contents of her handbag, still lying in a tumbled heap on the end of the bed. It was only as Amy saw the long, bronzed fingers sort through the untidy heap that she realised just what he had seen, exactly which item he was reaching for. Her heart stopped dead, then turned over sharply, making her head swim nauseously.

'Leave that alone...'

But once more she was too late. Even as she pushed herself into action, dashing forward across the room, Vincenzo's grip closed over the object of his search, lifting it swiftly. A tiny moan of despair escaped her as she saw him flick open the small, dark red passport and study what he found inside.

When he finally looked across at her again she felt the force of his glare as if it had been a physical blow, striking her hard in the chest and driving all the breath from her lungs that she gasped out loud in distress.

'Amy Redman,' he said, his voice so cold that she fully expected to see the two parts of her name form in letters of ice in the air between them, frozen solid. *'Amy Redman.'*

'What else would I put?' She tried bravado though her nerves were twisting into agonising knots, her legs trembling in terror. 'That's my name.'

'Your name—your real name—is Amy *Ravenelli.*'

If she thought she had ever seen him angry before, it had been as nothing when compared to the black, savage fury that now blazed in his eyes.

'That is your true name. The name you took when I married you. The name I gave you with my ring.'

If she'd spat on his father's grave, he couldn't have looked more offended. She'd truly trampled all over his pride in so many ways—over his male pride, the innate, essential pride that came from being an Italian, but most of all, the bone-deep, centuries-old pride of the Ravenelli family.

'It's not *my* name! It's yours—yours and your family's! It was never truly mine, not even on the day of our wedding. Because that wedding was a farce from start to finish. You never meant one of those vows even as you spoke them. It was all just to get your hands on that lousy ring!'

'And the bet, *carissima,*' Vincenzo reminded her, pure silken menace.

Dropping the passport back onto the bed in a gesture of absolute contempt he stood up slowly and elegantly.

'Don't forget the bet I made—that I could get you into my bed where my cousin's much-practised charms had failed.'

Don't forget.

The words seemed to form a knot in Amy's throat, threatening to choke of the air she needed to breathe. Don't forget? How could she ever forget the final humiliation, the ultimate cruelty of knowing that this man whom she had loved more than life itself, had only asked her to be his bride in a coldly selfish and most cynical manoeuvre aimed at seducing her where all else had failed?

'I haven't forgotten!' Desperately she hid pain behind defiance. 'But it seems that you have!'

A tiny, much-needed sense of triumph went a little way towards healing some of the agony the tore at her heart as she saw his faint frown of confusion, the questioning narrowing of his eyes.

Vincenzo Ravenelli looking unsure of himself. Now that was a new and very welcome experience!

'My memory of that day is only too clear,' Vincenzo stated coolly, every inch the Italian aristocrat looking down on some poor peasant well beneath his contempt.

'Then I have to admit to wondering just why you want either of us to keep to any of the promises we made that day. Why go to so much trouble to keep a bride you didn't even want in the first place, and must have been glad to get rid of as quickly and easily as you did?'

Something dangerous flared deep in the dark eyes, causing her to take a swift, nervous step backwards as if she had actually been subjected to a physical threat. And yet Vincenzo hadn't moved so much as an inch, not even raising an eyebrow, let alone a hand.

'I told you,' he stated coldly. 'No matter what you are, you are mine, and what is mine I keep. You are a Ravenelli by marriage, however that marriage came about, and it is my intention that you will stay a Ravenelli so long as it suits me.'

'Oh, now I know what it feels like to stand in the dock

and hear a sentence of life imprisonment handed out! Vincenzo, please…'

It wasn't until those dark, implacable eyes dropped to stare at her hands that Amy realised the way she had lifted them unthinkingly, holding them out towards him in an age-old gesture pleading for understanding. As soon as she realised what she had done, and felt that cold gaze fix on her, she hastily let them fall at her sides again, forming them into tightly clenched fists instead in an effort to control herself.

'If you give me my freedom, you can also have yours. Wouldn't we both be much happier with a chance to find someone else, someone new—someone who *loves* us and who we can—'

Something short and obviously brutal was flung at her in swift, harsh Italian, pulling her up sharp because she didn't understand a single word.

'What? Vincenzo, that isn't fair. You know I don't speak Italian! What are you saying?'

But Vincenzo wouldn't answer her. Instead he swung away from her, shoulders hunched, hands pushed deep into the pockets of his trousers, furious rejection of her stamped into every line of his long, straight back.

'Vincenzo! You can't do this! You have to tell me why you won't give me a divorce.'

That brought him whirling round again, proud head flung back, sensual mouth thinned to a cold hard line, the anger he had largely controlled until now blazing wildly out of control in those jet black eyes, stamped onto every taut muscle in his stunning face.

'Give you a divorce!' he echoed in stark incredulity. '*Give*—why the hell should I give you anything? By rights, if one of us should be doing it, I should be the one divorcing *you*!'

'What?'

Amy was definitely floundering now. A thick grey mist

was swirling around her, threatening to close in and shut off her thoughts, suffocating her completely.

'I don't understand…'

Blindly she reached out for the carved wooden end of the bed and grasped it tightly, holding on hard for support.

'What do you mean, you should be divorcing me?'

'Isn't it obvious?' Vincenzo flung the words into her white, shocked face as if even to speak them contaminated him. 'After all, who is the injured party here—and who's the one who broke her marriage vows?'

'Broke *her* marriage vows?'

Amy couldn't believe what she was hearing. Her fingers clenched even tighter over the bed end, clutching until the knuckles showed white. How, even in Vincenzo's arrogant, self-centred brain, could their situation become so turned around that he was claiming that he was the victim and she the guilty party?

'Vincenzo—just because I left you…'

'*No!*'

She had never heard his accent sound so hard and strong as it was on that single, explosive syllable.

'It is not *just* because you left me, though that is part of it. You say you want a divorce, but the truth is that *I* should be the one citing you—charging you with being unfaithful to me.'

'What?'

It was too much to take in. The room seemed to be whirling crazily round her, making her head spin, her stomach clench nauseously. She had to sit down. Her legs had turned to cotton wool and wouldn't support her any more. Nervelessly she sank down on to the bed, putting both hands flat on the blue quilt at her sides to support her.

She should be thankful that he had swallowed her story of a fictitious fiancé. Instead, she was horrified to hear he had taken it this far.

'You—I…'

'Oh, spare me the histrionics!' Vincenzo sneered, totally unmoved by the distress. 'Don't claim it's such a shock to you. You're the one who has turned up with a brand-new fiancé in tow. Your darling David.'

'But...'

Something exploded inside Amy's brain and she welcomed the fierce, liberating rush of anger that rocked her out of her stammering bemusement. How dared he think that she would reject her marriage vows so easily? She had meant them for life when she had said them.

'And I suppose *you're* so damn innocent!'

That wasn't possible. Not for a hot-blooded, highly sexually driven man like Vincenzo. A man who only had to click his fingers for willing, enthusiastic partners to fall at his feet, eager for his attentions. Hadn't she proved herself tonight that that white-hot sexual attraction that had once had her in its thrall was still there, lying in wait for her if she let down her guard for a second?

'You're not trying to claim that you've been celibate for the past four years? That in all that time there hasn't been anyone else?'

'There has been no one...'

'Oh, sure!' Amy scorned. 'No one that *mattered*! But plenty you could use and leave. Plenty of ships who passed in the night. Because, let's face it, Vincenzo, no woman ever means that much to you, does she?'

'Damn you, Amy!'

He moved then. Moved so swiftly that she barely saw him approach before he had caught hold of her arms and pulled her up from the bed, shaking her, not roughly, but in a fury of frustration.

'Damn you to hell! You're not listening. When I say no one, I mean *no one*!'

Amy knew that her shock must show in her face. That

her features had frozen and her mouth dropped slightly open.

'N-no one?' she managed at last, forcing the words out through lips that seemed to have turned to wood, they had become so stiff and unfeeling.

'No one,' Vincenzo repeated, releasing her at last so that she dropped back onto the bed, limp as a marionette with all its strings cut. 'I have not been to bed with another woman since I married you.'

So what did she do now?

Because she had to believe him. There was no room for any doubt in her mind, not when faced by that fiercely insistent declaration, the determination to convince her that was almost a physical force so that she imagined she could actually feel the heat of it on her face.

And she wanted to believe him. Foolishly, weakly, deep down inside there still lingered some tiny senseless, vulnerable little part of herself that wanted to be convinced that in this at least he was telling the truth. Because if he was, then…

No!

With a terrible effort she pulled herself up short, forced herself to face the truth. The *real* truth, no matter how much it hurt.

'So what do you want, a medal?'

Every last ounce of pain that she had endured since she had first met this man went into the words, all the bitterness she had experienced, the four long years of loneliness that seemed to last a lifetime. She had hurt for every second of those years, and now she couldn't hold back, wanting him to feel something of the same.

'So you've been "faithful" to me because of what—lack of opportunity? Big deal! There's more to a marriage than sex. There's caring and consideration. There's loving the other person so much that you put their needs before your own. And there's *honesty*…'

'Amy.' Her name was a sound of warning. One she was past heeding.

'You've told me there's no other woman who turns you on the way I do,' she rushed on headlong, staring at the wall past his shoulder, unable to meet his eyes. 'But that isn't enough. I want—I need more than that...'

'And you have found this with David?'

The honest answer to that was no. What she *truly* wanted was for Vincenzo to have loved her as she had once loved him. For him to have given her his heart as completely and unrestrainedly as she had given him hers.

But she could never have that.

'Amy!' Vincenzo was harshly insistent. 'Are you telling me that this David gives you what you want?'

'Yes!'

At last she forced herself to meet his eyes, recoiling from the pain of impacting with an onyx hardness, closed and shuttered as if steel blinds had come down behind them, cutting him off from her completely.

'Yes, yes, *yes*! David's what I want!' she said, desperate to convince him, seeing it as her only way out. 'The only man I want!'

Her words fell into a silence so profound that she thought even the sound of her drawing a raw, uneven breath into her aching lungs would splinter it around her, shattering the atmosphere like plate-glass when a stone was thrown into it. Then Vincenzo gave vent to one short, violent, and obviously obscene outburst of Italian before turning on his heel and marching towards the door.

Numbly Amy watched him go, unable to fully understand what she saw. Was that it? Was it all over?

Had Vincenzo finally given in?

She couldn't believe it if he had. And she was incapable of judging whether she had won or if the victory was actually his. Or perhaps both of them had lost, in their own way.

'Is that it?' she managed. 'You're leaving?'

'I think you have said everything I could possibly want to hear,' Vincenzo tossed over his shoulder at her.

She still couldn't breathe properly, and it was as she dragged in some much-needed air that she saw Vincenzo pause in the doorway and slowly turn back to face her. The darkness of the landing threw shadows onto his face, hollowing the lean planes of his cheeks, and making his eyes look like bottomless pits of black ice.

'You can choose to be with this David, say that he's the man you want,' he said slowly, his words and his tone combining to chill Amy's blood until it froze in her veins. 'But we both know that you are just deceiving yourself.'

Slowly those obsidian eyes raked over her trembling body, scorching it from top to toe in a ruthless, cold-hearted, unfeeling appraisal that made Amy feel physically violated all along the path his gaze had followed.

'No matter what happens, you are still my wife, and always will be. Even if you hold out for this divorce, it will change nothing, not deep down. I stamped my brand on you when I married you, and for the rest of your life you will carry it with you. However hard you try, I promise you will never be able to forget that you were once a Ravenelli bride.'

And the really appalling thing, Amy realised as she stood paralysed, watching him walk away from her, listening to his footsteps descending the stairs, was that she was very much afraid that he was right. Deep down inside, she knew that neither time nor space or the most concentrated effort on her part would ever manage to erase all memory of Vincenzo Ravenelli from her mind.

CHAPTER EIGHT

'I STAMPED my brand on you when I married you...'

The words Vincenzo had flung at her before he walked out the door seemed to have formed a sort of audio loop inside her head where they played over and over and over again, night and day, sleeping and waking, and there was no way at all that she could shut them up. The 'off' switch was broken, and it was impossible to wipe the tape, erase the ominous, terrifying declaration, escape its threatening implications.

'No!'

Amy tossed and turned restlessly, her sleep in the present broken by the memories of the past. With a cry of distress, she woke with a jolt, her eyes flying open to focus, blinking, on the window and the shaft of sunlight which was streaming through a crack in the curtain.

It was already morning, and yet she felt as if she had only just fallen asleep, barely managing any more than an hour or so's rest so that she was weary and jaded, far from ready to face Vincenzo again.

She would have to do so at some point. There was no avoiding the inevitable confrontation much as she would wish it. But even when she was up and dressed, ignoring the clothes in the wardrobe and opting instead for a simple blue T-shirt and cotton skirt that she had brought with her, her nerve failed her. Cravenly she stayed where she was, finding things to do with her hair, her make-up—anything other than emerge from her room and go downstairs.

She knew Vincenzo wouldn't wait for ever. Patience was not his greatest virtue, and what little he had would inevitably wear out fast. But the loud, imperious knock at the door still came much sooner than she had anticipated, and well before she was emotionally ready.

For a moment she considered ignoring it and pretending she wasn't there. A moment too long because even as she reconsidered the knock came again, louder this time, reverberating round the room.

'Are you going to stay sulking in your room all day?'

Sulking?

Incensed, Amy marched to the door and yanked it open. 'If you must know, I was doing my hair! I...'

'Looks fine to me,' Vincenzo spared her hair, lying loose and softly waving over her shoulder, a brief, critical glance. 'Though I'm forced to wonder if dear David will approve.'

'And just what is that supposed to mean?'

'Well it seems to me that if the way you were dressed when you first arrived, and with your hair dragged back into that unflattering style, is the sort of woman that being with David has turned you into then he really doesn't understand you at all.'

'And you do?'

Vincenzo's smile was dangerous, the gleam of triumph deep in the black eyes warning her that she had walked right into his trap.

'I *know* you, *cara*. I know the woman you become in my arms. The woman who comes alive in my bed. You can hide your real self under your so-English restrained tailoring, fasten that glorious hair back, conceal your sexuality in a hundred different ways, but you can't hide it from me. I know the real Amy—the woman who is Amy Ravenelli...'

'No, you don't!'

This was a path Amy didn't want to follow. It came too close to the subject of her dreams and the memories of that one, gloriously passionate night she had spent in Vincenzo's arms. Those memories, heated, erotic, yearning, had haunted her all night so that she had woken with her heart racing, drenched in sweat, her body aching and hungry.

And Vincenzo, tall and dark and lethally attractive in a black polo shirt and black jeans as he leaned against the doorframe, was the embodiment of the fantasies that had had her in their grip. With his hair crisp and damp from a shower, the scent of lemons and bergamot mixing in his cologne, and the sunlight gilding the bronzed skin, he was an assault on her senses just by existing.

'You know nothing about me! You only knew me for a few short days, less than a month from start to finish...'

'And I'd be willing to bet that in those "few short days" I came closer to the real woman than your precious David has in all the time you've been together.'

'Willing *to bet*?'

He couldn't have chosen to use any more incendiary words than those. With the image of the devastation of the first day of her marriage still lingering at the back of her thoughts, Amy was hypersensitive to them; just the use of the phrase set light to the touchpaper in her mind, with explosive effects.

'Willing to bet?' she repeated bitterly. 'And what, precisely, would you be prepared to wager on this one? Would that be worth—say—a stake as valuable as the Ravenelli ruby this time, or would that be selling your precious heirloom too cheaply? Do you only stake that on the conquest of a woman? On the taking of her virginity, the—'

'I did not bet on the *conquest* of anyone!'

Vincenzo's voice hadn't lifted above conversational level, but there was a vicious savagery in his tone, a violence only barely controlled that made his response more frightening than if he had actually yelled at her.

But Amy was past caring.

'No, you had more confidence in your own seduction technique than that. You knew you wouldn't have to conquer anyone—just turn on the famed Ravenelli charm and the poor gullible fool would fall flat at your feet. But I'll bet the one thing you hadn't bargained on was that I would hold out for marriage. That must have given you pause, made you think. Was it worth it, Cenzo?'

Deliberately she used the old affectionate term, lacing it with burning acid, and she felt a glow of triumph as she saw his proud head go back sharply and knew that her barb had hit its mark.

'You said you'd give the world—do anything you could to get it back. But was it worth tying yourself in marriage to a woman you didn't love, a woman who hates you, in order to regain your precious ruby ring?'

'If you want to know the truth, then no, it wasn't,' he stated flatly.

Well, she'd asked for it. So she had no right to complain if his words were like a stab of ice in her heart, tearing at the already wounded tissues.

'But I'm forced to wonder,' Vincenzo continued savagely, 'whether you'd recognise the truth if you heard it.'

'You once told me…'

'That I never lie,' he finished for her when she couldn't complete the sentence. 'And I never have.'

'You…'

But her voice failed her once again. She couldn't accuse him of lying to her by declaring that he loved her, because she had to admit that he had never, ever, claimed such a thing. Even when he had asked her to marry him, he had only said that he wanted her more than any other woman, that he hungered for her physically, and that was something she had always known, and still knew to be the truth.

It was Amy herself who, blinded by her own feeling, had taken that declaration to mean something else. She had believed that by 'wanting' he had meant loving, and so her whole world had collapsed in on her when she had found out just how wrong she had been.

'Can your beloved David say as much?' Vincenzo questioned softly, a deadly menace in his tone making her skin crawl with nerves. 'Or can you?'

Amy had had enough.

'Oh, leave me alone! Go away and leave me in peace, can't you?'

She made a move to shut the door, only to have it forestalled by Vincenzo's quick response, the way his hand came out to block the action, one elegantly booted foot being planted firmly in the doorway, keeping it open.

'Oh, no, you don't, *carissima!*' he declared. 'You slammed a door in my face once. I do not intend to let you repeat the insult. Besides, if you run now, you will miss out on hearing the good news I have for you.'

That stopped Amy's impetus towards angry reaction, stilling her hand on the door and leaving her standing staring in amazement.

'Good news?' she stammered in disbelief. 'What good news?'

Had something happened overnight? Something she was unaware of? Could Vincenzo possibly have changed his mind?

No, she couldn't let herself think that. She didn't dare even to hope for it. When Vincenzo made up his mind it usually stayed made up. And he had been so determined to make her suffer last night.

'I've been thinking.'

Nothing in Vincenzo's face gave any indication of the way this was leading, so that Amy felt as if she was groping desperately in the dark.

'And?' she prompted nervously when his pause dragged on, stretching her nerves to screaming pitch.

'And I have reconsidered slightly.'

Reconsidered. Amy's heart leapt in sudden excitement. Could it be that after all he was prepared to co-operate?

'You'll agree to a divorce?'

'I'm not saying that.'

Releasing his hold on the door, he straightened up slowly, flexing his shoulders before waving an autocratic hand to take in her belongings scattered around the blue and cream bedroom.

'Get packed. You're going home.'

'Home?' Amy echoed, shocked by his dismissive tone and totally at a loss as to where this conversation was going. 'But...'

'Go home,' Vincenzo repeated, 'and I will follow you in a few days time. I will meet your darling David...'

'No!' Amy protested wildly, her heart quailing inside her just at the thought of her subterfuge being blown wide open. 'You can't do that! You mustn't!'

Vincenzo shrugged off her interjection, strolling into the room and throwing himself into a chair, leaning back in it, long legs crossed at the ankles, bronze-skinned hands steepled underneath his firm jaw.

'I want to see this David for myself. Learn more about him. Where did you first encounter him, for example?'

'I—I work for him, as his secretary.' She gave the information reluctantly. 'He runs a building firm in Charnham.'

'I see.'

It was like watching a computer at work, taking in the facts, sorting through them, filing them away for future reference. And it made the nerves in her stomach twist painfully, wondering just what use he might put them to.

'Vincenzo...'

She forced herself to walk towards him, keeping a tight grip on herself to ensure that her legs were steady, her face expressionless.

'Why, exactly, do you want to see David?'

'Isn't it obvious? I want to see what he can offer you; how he feels about you. If he is the right man for you, if he can really give you more than I can, then I will stand aside. I will sign the papers, give you a divorce.'

'You will!' Amy couldn't believe what she was hearing. 'Do you mean this? Really mean it?'

A slight inclination of his dark head indicated agreement, Vincenzo's black eyes hooded and inscrutable.

'But only if he is the right man.'

For the first time, an edge of unease crept into Amy's newfound delight.

'And if he's not?'

A cutting gesture of one elegant hand made it only too plain what was in Vincenzo's mind.

'No divorce. Ever.'

'But…' Amy began, but Vincenzo got to his feet again, indicating that in his opinion, the conversation was at an end.

'Pack your things,' he commanded. 'Go home. I will come to you.'

'But what if David finds out who you are? What will I tell him?'

Polished jet eyes bored into her face with the fierce power of a laser beam, seeming to reach right into her soul and read what was on it.

'You have already told him I am someone you met in Venice. It would probably be best to stick to that. You can leave the rest to me. Our true relationship will be our own little secret, one that no one need find out about unless I decide otherwise.'

CHAPTER NINE

ANOTHER day and still no message from Vincenzo.

Amy sighed as she pushed a sheaf of papers into a folder in the filing cabinet and then slammed the drawer shut with a resounding clang.

The waiting was the worst. Surely even having Vincenzo here, in person, watching everything she did couldn't be as bad as this not knowing. At least then she would understand exactly what she was dealing with, while this...

The next sigh was deeper, her blue eyes clouded, hands pushed into the pockets of her tailored navy dress, as she stared out of the window at the hills and streets of the small northern English town, so different from the sunlit elegance of Venice. This felt unnervingly like waiting for the executioner's axe to fall, never quite knowing when the blow would come.

It was two weeks since she had last seen Vincenzo. Two weeks in which she hadn't heard a thing. Not a phone call, an e-mail, not even a postcard. He might as well have vanished into the ether for all the communication she had had with him. If this went on much longer, she was going to have to break her self-imposed rule of not contacting him herself. Her nerves were shot to ribbons as it was. Any further delay and she felt she would crack altogether.

The sound of footsteps coming down the corridor, a familiar voice, sent Amy hurrying to her desk. It wouldn't do for David to find her daydreaming like this. He had already noted her increasingly abstracted moods ever since her return from Italy. Any more and she was sure he was going to start asking questions she would find it extremely difficult to answer.

'I think we'll find her in here,' she heard David saying as she hastily brought up a file at random on her computer screen. 'She won't be expecting to see you.'

Expecting to see who? She was sure that the office diary was empty, and she had made no personal appointments for this afternoon. Work time was for work, and she always kept scrupulously to that.

'Ah, there you are!'

David's greeting brought her eyes to him just as he came through the door, a broad smile on his narrow face under the slightly thinning fair hair.

'I have a surprise for you.'

'Surprise?'

Amy had just time to form the question, a faint frown drawing her brows together, before he moved completely into the room and his place in the doorway was taken by another man.

A taller, darker, broader man. A man whose steel grey suit and immaculate white shirt shrieked—no, murmured— of perfect designer elegance and the money to buy it. A man whose coal-black hair and eyes had haunted her dreams by night and her thoughts by day until she was thoroughly distracted and limp as an over-washed dish-cloth. A man whose appearance she had both longed for and dreaded fearfully over the past fourteen days.

'*Buon giorno*, Amy.'

'S-signor Ravenelli...'

It took an effort to make her voice work, and even when she managed to get the greeting out she still sounded like someone whose voice was rusty as a result of a bad cold and a very sore throat indeed.

Who did he think he was, strolling in here as if he owned the place? In the frankly uninspired beige and brown surroundings of her office, his height and colouring, the sleek styling of his clothes, looked both sophisticated and exotic.

Too showy, too expensive, Amy told herself. Just too damn much, altogether.

'I wasn't expecting to see you…' she continued inanely, earning herself a small, wicked grin and a black eyebrow lifted just a fraction in mocking acknowledgement of her obvious consternation.

She could only be thankful that Vincenzo was still standing slightly behind David so that the other man could see nothing of his expression or the taunting gleam in the deep, onyx eyes.

'You didn't tell me that Signor Ravenelli was planning on investing in premises in Britain.'

David's reproof was mild, but it was a reproach all the same. And Amy thought she could guess why. Given his admiration of Vincenzo's business acumen and success, an admiration that he had expressed on more than one occasion since her return, she knew that he would have been delighted to think that he would have an opportunity to meet the Italian. And he would have much preferred to have had an opportunity to prepare for it.

As she would have done, Amy reflected with a fulminating glare slanted in Vincenzo's direction.

A glare that he deflected with an easy smile, seeming to direct its force right back at her as he murmured smoothly, 'I didn't tell Amy anything about it. In fact, I didn't make up my mind until a couple of days ago. But when I did, it seemed logical that I should get in touch with her again. She'd told me that she worked for a building firm, and naturally I shall need to employ someone to adapt the premises I acquire to fit my requirements.'

'Naturally.'

Amy heard David's smiling agreement with an uneasy mixture of relief and horror. Clever, clever Vincenzo! He had somehow sussed out the fact that David's business was central to his life. To suggest using that company, adding to its profits, was guaranteed to win his approval, his co-operation in any matter he chose to raise.

'We didn't actually arrange any exact date, did we, Amy? It was simply an understanding that when I was next in England I would call and say hello if I had the time.'

'It—it was a very fluid arrangement,' Amy managed, regaining some control over thoughts that Vincenzo's unexpected appearance had thrown into total chaos. 'Nothing definite. Just if he happened to be passing.'

That devilish grin grew wider, quirking the beautiful mouth up at one corner as, realising her own mistake, Amy bit down hard on her own lower lip, silently cursing her foolishness. The likelihood of anyone 'just passing' Charnham, one of the smallest towns in this part of West Yorkshire, was so far-fetched as to be downright farcical. No one made a detour here unless they had a particular reason to do so.

'Would you like coffee?' she managed, wincing at the sound of her own voice, the brittle gaiety she projected that was so obviously artificial and forced.

'That would be good.' Thankfully she heard Vincenzo follow her lead. 'It's been quite a drive from the airport.'

Amy was relieved to escape from the room to fetch water for the filter machine. It gave her the opportunity to draw in several deep, much-needed, calming breaths of air and run her wrists under the cold tap in an effort to control her racing pulse.

No wonder Vincenzo had delayed his arrival for the past fortnight. He must have had to hunt around to find the address of David's office in the first place. She was sure she'd never given him anything more than the minimum of basic information when she was in Italy. She was lucky that David's inbuilt admiration for anyone who made a fortune in business as Vincenzo had, would probably keep his conversation to the matter of work and contracts or investment. That way, hopefully they would avoid any awkward questions.

But even so she didn't dare to leave them alone together for too long. Vincenzo's declaration that, 'I never, ever lie,' now seemed like a warning that, if challenged, he would reveal everything to David and to hell with the consequences.

Heart thudding frantically, her mind a whirl of apprehension, Amy hurried back to the office, suddenly fearful of what might have happened in her absence.

Her worst fears were confirmed when she pushed open the door to hear David saying casually, 'And so where are you staying? Briar Court, I presume—or perhaps that new five-star place out of town?'

'Neither of those,' Vincenzo returned easily enough, but something about his tone, a bubbling undercurrent of dark amusement gave a hint of warning, setting all the tiny hairs on the back of Amy's neck quivering in tension like the response of a nervous cat. 'Didn't Amy tell you?'

The filter jug of water slid awkwardly in Amy's suddenly nerveless grasp, landing on the hot plate with a distinct crash. With an effort she controlled her instinctive impulse to whirl round in panic and confront him openly.

'Didn't I tell him what?' she managed, staring fixedly at the wall as she struggled to control her breathing.

'About our arrangement.'

The cruel amusement had definitely intensified now, though Amy was sure that it was only her own senses, already on overdrive where Vincenzo was concerned, that picked it up. David seemed stolidly unaware of any undercurrents, only curious to know about the subject under discussion.

'And what arrangement is that?' he asked now.

'Shall I explain, Amy, or will you?' Vincenzo's question had just the right degree of courtesy, of apparent consideration for her feelings.

Somehow managing to find the control to delay until she had flicked the switch to start the coffee bubbling, Amy turned slowly to face Vincenzo again, her chin coming up, her eyes widening as she silently defied him to do his worst. She didn't know what was in that coolly calculating mind, but she was pretty sure she was about to find out.

'Why don't you tell him?' she murmured with a sweetness so blatantly false that she was surprised to find that drops of acid didn't fall onto the carpet and eat it away at her feet. 'Since you can obviously explain it more clearly than I could.'

A tiny flicker of a smile, the faintest inclination of his glossy dark head acknowledged admiration for her unspoken challenge. But that did nothing to ease the uncomfortably ragged beat of her pulse, the sudden dryness of her mouth as she waited for him to elaborate on just what he had in mind.

'It's like this...'

Vincenzo turned his attention to David, his tone altering, sliding into an affable, relaxed, man-to-man tone, his smile calculated to convince the other man that he had nothing underhand in mind.

'When I told Amy that I was coming to England for a couple of months, I also told her how much I detest living in hotels. Even the very best of them have an institutional nature, an impersonal approach that means I can't fully relax at the end of a long working day. Then there's the fact that, staying in an hotel, you get no chance to learn how the people in the country you're visiting really live. What their homes are like, their lives, their interests...'

Their homes. As the words sank in ominously, Amy shifted nervously from one foot to another, biting down hard on her lower lip in a frantic attempt to hold back the cry of protest that almost escaped her. She had the disturbing feeling that she knew exactly where this conversation was going, and she didn't like it one bit. But to object now, with Vincenzo fully launched on his wickedly plausible explanation, would only make matters worse, adding fuel to the fire of David's suspicions just when she wanted to extinguish them.

'So when we discovered that by a remarkable coincidence my business in England would probably bring me here, to Charnham, to Amy's home town, she offered me the perfect solution.'

Remarkable coincidence, indeed! Amy thought privately, hating the gleam in Vincenzo's eyes.

'As you know, my flat has a spare room standing empty…' she broke in sharply, taking control of the conversation herself.

Vincenzo might have the upper hand at the moment, but that didn't mean she had to let him have everything his own way. At least if she took the initiative she would prove that she wasn't just some sort of a carpet that he could trample all over, wiping the soles of his polished, handmade boots on her whenever he felt like it.

'So I offered Mr Ravenelli the use of it—for a reasonable rent.'

She couldn't resist a swift sidelong glance at Vincenzo as she added the final, pointed phrase, then wished she hadn't because another of those slight inclinations of his head in approval made it appear far too much as if they were conspirators, in this together, for her liking.

'What a practical solution.'

The shrill of the telephone from the next room, David's office, had him turning his head in that direction.

'I'll get that,' he said when Amy made a move to go and answer it. 'You see to the coffees.'

With David at his desk, and the security of the closed door between them, Amy rounded on Vincenzo, blue eyes flashing angry fire.

'My room!' she exclaimed furiously. 'You're staying in

my spare room! In my home! You're pushing things, Vincenzo. We had no such agreement. I never offered…'

'Oh, but you did,' he returned with an imperturbable little smile. 'Just now you offered me the use of your spare room "for a reasonable rent".' Tauntingly, he repeated her own words back to her. 'I was actually about to suggest that you had offered to help me find a house to let locally.'

Finding herself totally checkmated, Amy could only decide that, in this case, discretion was definitely the better part of valour, and she set herself to pouring the coffees with unnecessary concentration. She had no way of knowing whether Vincenzo had had any such thing in mind, and that he had simply opened a door that she had blindly walked through.

But it was obvious that she had been outmanoeuvred by an expert and there was nothing she could do about it. She could only hope that if she had a quiet word with David later, he would understand her concern at having a man she supposedly hardly knew sharing her home and would offer to have a word with Vincenzo in order to get him to change his mind.

Unfortunately, David failed to see her point of view.

'I understand your feelings, Amy,' he said when, using the excuse of some papers she needed signing, she raised the matter with him in the privacy of his office. 'But I don't think you need to worry. Didn't you notice his hands?'

'His hands?' Amy echoed in bewilderment. What did Vincenzo's hands have to do with anything?

'He's wearing a wedding ring,' David explained patiently. 'He's a married man. So I hardly think you need to worry about his behaviour when he's with you.'

A married man! Amy didn't know whether to laugh or give in to the tears of sheer frustration that were burning in her eyes. Of course she knew that dreadful man was married!

She couldn't believe the appalling irony that David

thought her peace of mind had been earned by the band of gold that was her own worst nightmare. But of course, David was thinking once again of the potential benefits to his company of Vincenzo's presence in Charnham. With Amy acting as hostess, her employer would have the perfect excuse to call round, socialise with him.

Which added another, further complication to her own problems. David's firm had not been doing too well recently. Any business Vincenzo could put their way would be more than welcome. More than that.

In fact, aside from the Randerson contract that David had rung to tell her about so inopportunely in Venice, they had no business lined up for the future. Vincenzo's interest could save them from bankruptcy. But equally, one false move to alienate him would mean that she was out of a much-needed job and once more hunting for employment. It was not a comfortable feeling.

And as the days passed, that feeling grew worse, closing round her until she felt as if she was being slowly suffocated, unable to breathe.

With Vincenzo there in her life, living in her home, it seemed as if her existence was not her own. If she turned round he was there, watching every move she made. If she went into the kitchen, he was making coffee or a snack.

Even her bathroom was permeated by the tangy, evocative scent of his male toiletries. Just to go in there was to awaken unwanted memories of long-ago days when she had been held so close to the powerful strength of his hard male body, breathing that same sensual aroma mixed with the more intimate, personal scent of his skin.

It was there in her nostrils when she went to bed at night, so it was no wonder that her dreams were filled with wild, tormenting images, replaying over and over again the one hot night she had spent in Vincenzo's bed. Her wedding night. As a result she slept restlessly and uncomfortably, waking in a tangle of sheets, her heart pounding, her body slick with perspiration, an empty ache of longing burning cruelly at the juncture of her thighs.

It had been like this four years before, when she had first left Vincenzo. She had fled back to England, hiding there like some wounded animal seeking sanctuary from the hunters. She had never expected that Vincenzo would come after her, knocking at her door...

'Amy...Amy?'

It took several moments to realise that the voice was not part of her dreams. That the knocking at her door was real.

Her eyes flew open on a cry of shock. The subject of her memories stood beside the bed, a dark, disturbing shape in the shadows of just before dawn.

'What are you doing in my room?'

The thoughtless question earned her a scowl of reproof.

'I had to wake you. You cried out in your sleep, and you were tossing around so much I thought you might throw yourself out of bed. You must have been in the grip of nightmare.'

She still was, Amy reflected. Only this time it was a waking dream. This time, the tall, strong figure confronting her was real, not just some figment of her imagination. Vincenzo's black hair was ruffled from sleep, his bronzed chest bare, his only covering a pair of black pyjama bottoms that might have covered the length and power of his legs, but they certainly didn't conceal it.

Amy's mouth was uncomfortably dry, and she had to swallow hard to ease the sudden tension in her throat. She was suddenly a prey to a shockingly forceful desire, a wild, erotic image centering on catching hold of the long, tanned arm that was so temptingly close. So close that she could almost feel the brush of the silky dark hairs, inhale the warm scent of his skin, musky with the aftermath of sleep.

She could just reach out and fasten her hand around his wrist...pull him into bed with her...kiss that sleep-softened mouth...

No! A short, brutal little struggle restored her mental balance again. But she wasn't totally free of the sensual memories of her wedding night yet.

'A nightmare…' she echoed, on a long despondent sigh. 'Yes…'

In spite of herself she shivered miserably, unable to shrug off the bitter memories.

'Amy!'

Vincenzo's voice was soft and to her horror he came to sit on the bed beside her, one strong arm coming round her shoulder, drawing her close.

'What is it that frightened you?'

You frightened me, would have been the honest answer, but she couldn't bring herself to say it. She couldn't say anything, fearful of shattering the unexpectedly gentle mood of the moment.

She just wanted to be held—if only for a moment. Held and comforted. The weight and warmth of Vincenzo's arm around her, his body close to hers, was soothing after the terrors of her dreams. With the instinctive reaction of a small child seeking comfort, she cuddled closer, resting her head on his chest.

'Amy?'

His voice was even gentler now and she felt the soft drift of his mouth across her hair in a delicate caress as he muttered something in low-voiced Italian.

'What did you say?' she asked huskily and felt him stiffen slightly against her.

'That you have no need to worry,' he translated with obvious reluctance. 'That if you need me I will stay until you fall asleep. That I will watch over you and protect you from the demons of the night.'

She was tempted. Dear God, but she was tempted. Every cell in her body was begging her to abandon herself to the protection of his arms, to indulge in the security he seemed to offer. But her mind and every trace of self protection she possessed warned her that that security was no more than a lie.

'Why did you come after me?' It wasn't what she'd meant to say but somehow the question slid out past defences weakened by the comfort of his presence. 'When I left you after our marriage, you said you never wanted to see me again, so why did you follow me?'

For a long moment she thought he wasn't going to answer, but just as she was about to give up on the idea he gave a faint sigh and rubbed the back of his free hand across his forehead in a gesture of unexpected weariness.

'Because I couldn't help myself,' he answered on a note of self-deprecation. 'And I wanted to explain.'

'Explain?'

Amy pulled herself up on the pillows so that she could look into his shadowed face, finding it impossible to read in the moonlight.

'Explain what?'

'About the bet.'

The word was like a knife in her heart. But even as she opened her mouth to launch into an attack, wanting to turn the pain back on him, something stopped her.

She didn't know what it was; whether it was the darkness or the lateness of the hour that stopped her. This moment felt like a tiny sliver of space suspended out of normal time. It seemed almost unreal, as if nothing they did in it really mattered, or would have any repercussions later.

'What would you have said?'

Vincenzo followed her lead with intuitive empathy.

'That when Sal suggested the idea, it had nothing to do with you as a person. I hadn't even met you then.'

'And when you did?'

'To tell you the truth, I forgot all about the damn bet. It was only later that I remembered…'

'And you didn't think that perhaps it might be more moral to tell me—or to let me go?'

'No!'

The shake of his head was as violent as his tone.

'I couldn't let you go. I'd never seen anyone like you. Never met anyone who knocked me for six the way you did.'

'Convenient for you.' Bitterness made her voice burn. 'That way, you could mix business with pleasure—get your kicks and still win back the ruby. It would have been so much harder if I'd repelled you.'

'I told you, it wasn't like that. I *wanted* you so badly.'

'You wanted the ruby.' Wrenching herself away from him, Amy sat up suddenly, looking straight into his face. 'Which did you want the most?'

The way his expression changed, closing up on her, his hesitation, told their own story. Her heart seemed to crack open inside her. Did she really need an answer?

'I wanted the ruby,' he confirmed. 'But—'

'But you were greedy,' Amy finished for him. 'What you really wanted was both. Well, fifty per cent isn't a bad return. You've got the ring; you'll have to settle for that.'

'Amy…'

'No!'

He'd almost managed it. Almost deceived her into thinking that perhaps she'd got him wrong, that perhaps… No, she mustn't allow herself the weakness of even thinking that way.

'Get out!' she flung at him. 'Get out and leave me alone.'

Immediately the long body stiffened into a line of cold rejection. The arm around her was snatched away; Vincenzo got to his feet in one swift, lithe movement.

'Willingly,' he muttered, cold and clipped and totally hostile and, turning on his heel, he marched from the room.

Amy regretted her hard words as soon as they were out. He had come to her room out of concern. He had offered her comfort. He could quite easily have simply ignored the disturbed cries she had made in her sleep.

Vincenzo! She tried to call after him but her voice failed her, producing only an inaudible croak.

'Vincenzo!' She tried again, but it was too late. His long strides had already taken him down the landing and into his own room.

The sound of his door banging shut seemed to echo down through the years, bringing with it the memory of the only other time Vincenzo had been in England and she had told him to go to hell.

He hadn't given up, even after she'd slammed the door in his face. He'd banged his fist hard against the wood, put his finger on the bell and left it there. But eventually, when she'd threatened to send for the police, he'd seen the wisdom of discretion and left.

But he hadn't actually conceded defeat, not really. Because the last words he'd flung at her were still branded into her soul. Etched there in letters of fire.

'I will not come to you again, *moglie mia*. The next time *you* will come to me.'

Her relationship with Vincenzo was over, dead, Amy told herself desperately, fighting back the tears that stung her eyes. It had been that way for years.

She was ready to begin a new way of life, ready to look to the future. So why, *why* would her weak, foolish thoughts keep on returning to the past?

'Why?' she muttered aloud. 'Why, why, why?'

And the dark silence of the night held no possible answer except for the one she didn't dare to face, knowing it would tear her apart if she did so.

CHAPTER TEN

'AMY, are you *ever* going to give me an answer to my question?'

For a few fraught moments Amy couldn't remember just what question David meant, and she had opened her mouth to ask for elucidation when realisation had her closing it again in shock, horrified at the terrible mistake she had almost made.

'I—I need time to think,' she hedged awkwardly, concentrating fiercely on the flowers she was arranging, and praying that the extravagant foliage hide the way all colour had faded from her cheeks, leaving her looking pale and strained.

David's sigh was a perfect blend of exasperation and resigned patience, rapidly wearing thin at the edges.

'Just how long do you plan on keeping me waiting? It was only an invitation to dinner.'

'I know!'

Amy pushed the last rose into the vase with such force that its delicate stalk broke under the pressure, the rich, red velvet head drooping over sadly.

It looked just the way she felt, she reflected unhappily. Limp and beaten down, and thoroughly dejected.

Three weeks of Vincenzo's presence in her life had done that to her. Three weeks of having to watch every move, censor every sentence she spoke. Three weeks of not daring to breathe, terrified of putting a foot wrong. Of going to bed at night exhausted and drained as a result of constantly worrying that today might be the day she betrayed herself by a word or a gesture. And waking up again every bit as tired as before, after long, restless hours spent staring at the ceiling, reviewing the day in the vain hope that she might actually get some sleep.

And then David had suddenly decided to complicate matters, albeit unknowingly. First with the unexpected dinner invitation and now the roses he had arrived at her flat to present her with this afternoon. The flowers in particular were so unlike him that they'd knocked her off balance completely.

'I don't mean to mess you about, David...'

Unable to pretend that the roses needed her attention any more, she swung round to face him, forcing what she hoped was an appeasing smile on to her face.

'But it's just that I'm not sure I'm quite ready for this. With...'

Shuddering in shock, she hastily gulped down the words she had been about to say.

With one broken marriage behind me...

Dear God, she had come so close to giving herself away!

There was no way she could expect David to understand the foolish mistake her marriage had been. He wasn't the sort of man to let any emotion run away with him. He seemed to have been born middle-aged, and 'sensible' was very definitely his middle name.

'With?' David prompted when she remained lost in thought, leaving the revealing sentence hanging in the air.

'With—' Amy hunted frantically for something to fill the uncomfortable space. 'With—with work being so pressurised lately, I've hardly had time to breathe, let alone think!'

Mentioning work had been the right idea, distracting David instantly. Vincenzo had been as good as his word. Already, several major projects were in the pipeline, and David's attention focused on them night and day.

'We both have,' he conceded. 'It's been a difficult time but I think it's finally paying off. We'll be able to look to the future.'

'I'd like that.'

It came out on a sigh, putting more emphasis than she had meant onto the words. If only she *could* think about a future. A time when her own position was decided, when Vincenzo had given her her freedom and gone back to Italy, leaving her in peace.

'Is that your answer?' David pounced on her abstracted reply, making her realise her mistake just a moment too late. 'That we have a future together?'

'I—no—I mean...David, please don't push me!'

It would be so much easier if she could say yes. If she could have turned the relationship she had claimed to have with her boss into something real. She was comfortable with him, they had worked together well for three years and they shared interests in music and the theatre. But there was no *love*—and there never could be.

Coming to her side, David took her hand in his.

'Promise me you'll think about it,' he murmured in her ear, twisting her in his arms so that they were face to face. 'We get along well together in everything else. Isn't it time we found out if we're compatible in other ways?'

Taken completely aback, Amy rocked slightly on suddenly unsteady feet, not at all prepared to answer that question.

'But—but, David—I...' she began, with no idea as to how she was going to continue.

But she was saved from having to answer by the slam of a door, and a moment later Vincenzo strolled into the room.

'Oh, *scusi*!'

His start of surprise, his careful apology when he saw her in David's arms, were perfect. So why should Amy's suspicions be raised instantly, her reaction instinctive like the lifting of the hackles on the neck of a defensive cat facing an intruder into its territory?

Because it was just *too* perfect. Because it made her feel

that it was calculated to give exactly the impression he wanted.

'No problem.' She managed to keep her voice calm, her body still. At the beginning, when Vincenzo had first moved into her home, she had reacted almost with panic to his every appearance.

Well, not this time, she resolved. Behaviour like that was just playing right into Vincenzo's hands.

So she stayed right where she was, meeting the speculative glance of those dark, deep-set eyes with defiance, before she eased herself away.

'I was just about to make some tea. Would you like some?'

'I'd love some.'

Her question had been addressed to David, but it was Vincenzo who answered, throwing himself down in one of the deep brown velvet-covered chairs and stretching lazily.

'It's warm out there, and I'm very thirsty.'

Get your own tea, Amy was tempted to snap, but she bit the words back hastily. She was not going to let Vincenzo get to her any more. In fact, she was not even going to *notice* him any more. She was just going to get on with her life and not let him be any part of it.

That was easier said than done, especially when Vincenzo, casually dressed in a crisp white polo shirt and elderly denim jeans, wandered into the kitchen after her.

'Need any help?'

'To make tea?' Amy scorned. 'No.'

Those jeans were so worn that they clung to the strong lines of his body in a way that was practically indecent, and the contrast of the pristine white shirt with the glowing bronze of his skin make her heart kick in her chest in response. Even such sunshine as the early English summer had brought, mild and brief compared to the heat of his native land, had deepened the year-round tan he wore naturally. With his glossy dark hair and brilliant eyes, he appeared like an exotic wild predator in the midst of a bunch of dowdy sparrows.

'I'll get the mugs anyway.'

'You can do what you like.'

She didn't care if she sounded ungracious. She felt ungracious, and she was damn sure he knew exactly why. Knew it and was playing on it quite deliberately.

And the narrow confines of her small galley kitchen were not the best place to try and go through even the simple procedure of making a cup of tea in close proximity to a devastating male like Vincenzo. Every one of Amy's senses seemed to be on red alert, her eyes having to be dragged away from the vibrant masculine presence of him, her skin tingling as if undergoing an electric shock if she so much as brushed past him.

She tried to close her ears to the sound of his soft baritone humming as he went about his task, hold her breath against the scent of sun, fresh air and clean, warm skin that pervaded the atmosphere. Her own soft blue cotton dress seemed to brush over her sensitised skin in a way that made her shiver in response.

'That colour doesn't suit you,' Vincenzo said suddenly, seeming to pick up on her thoughts in a way that was thoroughly unnerving.

'David thinks it looks very smart,' Amy retorted, dumping biscuits on a plate with such force that two of them broke in half.

'Then David has no taste. With your colouring you look much better in richer, deeper colours, red or purple or—'

'Or the sort of thing you once bought me!'

'Exactly.'

His smile mocked her prickly response.

'Why do you think I bought them for you?'

'Well frankly, I think they were over the top and quite unsuitable for an English climate.'

Hopefully the force of her reply hid the twisting pang of

regret that she couldn't suppress at the thought of the beautiful, jewel-coloured clothes she had left behind, confined to the wardrobe in the house in Venice.

'They're just not me.'

'They're certainly not the you I've seen since I came to England,' Vincenzo returned sardonically. 'That dress must be the closest to anything bright that you've worn in weeks. And I don't believe I've seen you with your hair any way but in that appallingly tight style once.'

The scowling glance he directed at the smooth chignon in which Amy's rich dark hair was confined expressed his disapproval far more eloquently than words could ever do.

'The way I dress has nothing to do with you! I wear what I like, and I choose my clothes to suit the woman I am.'

'So you actually *choose* to look like a repressed spinster?' Disbelief rang in his voice. 'And hide away the warm, sensual woman I know really exists? That kettle's boiling.'

'I'm well aware of that!'

Amy snatched up the kettle, her abrupt, jerky movements perfectly mirroring the uncomfortable state of her thoughts.

'You know nothing about me!' she raged on, splashing boiling water into the teapot with reckless abandon. 'And I'm not *hiding* anything! I am simply— *Ouch!*'

She broke off on a cry of shock as an unwise movement made the hot water splatter onto her hand, scalding it painfully.

'Amy, *cara!*'

Reacting with instinctive speed, Vincenzo's arms came round her, swinging her in an arc towards the sink. Pulling the kettle from her hand, he pushed her injured fingers under the cold tap, turning it on with full force as he did so. Biting her lip against the discomfort, Amy gave a small, sobbing cry of relief as the icy water poured over her hand, soothing it immediately.

But the sensations rushing through the rest of her body were very different. *Soothed* was the exact opposite of the way his touch made her feel. It was as if tiny rivulets of fire were spreading out from the point where his fingers were resting, searing her delicate skin with a sensation far more disturbing than the sting of her injury. She was achingly, hungrily, shockingly alive.

His nearness, the feel of that muscular body so close to hers, firm and hard under the white shirt, was almost more than she could bear. She could breathe in the scent of him with a sensuality that rocked her balance; even the soft sound of his breathing played havoc with her already tightly stretched nerves.

'I'm—I'm okay,' she said hastily, struggling for the composure not to wrench away from him. 'You can let me go now.'

His response was slow in coming and when she heard it she was overwhelmed by a devastating impulse to give in to the weak tears that were pricking at her eyes.

'I don't want to,' Vincenzo said simply, softly. 'I don't want to let you go.'

'Well, you *have* to!' Amy hissed through clenched teeth, stiffening every muscle into tight rejection of the insidious, snaking appeal of just being close to him, that seemed to coil round her like scented smoke.

'No, I don't,' he contradicted softly. 'On our wedding day, I took you as mine—to have and to hold. You may be able to forget those vows so easily but—'

'I haven't forgotten them!

It was so cruelly tempting. His mouth was so close to hers. All she had to do was to lift her face, tilt her chin just so… Only the scream of her nerves in recognition of the danger she was in held her back, forcing her to face reality.

'But David is just next door; he might come in at any moment.'

Too late she saw how the way she had phrased things

could seem to imply that her rejection of him was based solely on that fear. And of course, Vincenzo, being the man he was, pounced on that small weakness immediately.

'If that's all that's troubling you, then tell him. Come with me right now and we'll tell him the truth together...'

He had his hand in her uninjured one, had even led her partway towards the door before reality returned in full, forcing her to dig in her heels and pull him to a halt.

'I don't want to tell David anything!'

'He has to know some time.'

Vincenzo shrugged off her protest with a casual indifference that had her clenching her fists against the urge to scream with frustration.

'He doesn't have to know a damn thing! Because there is nothing for him to know! I have nothing—get that—*nothing* to tell him!'

The look her turned on her was pure scorn, contempt blazing in the coal black depths of his eyes.

'Coward,' he murmured with a silky toned disdain that still managed to seem to scrape away a protective layer of her skin, leaving her feeling raw and vulnerable.

'Cowardice has nothing to do with it.'

A quick twist of her wrist freed her from his unexpectedly loosened grasp.

'But a very thick skin and total refusal to accept the truth on your part has. *I do not want to be with you.*'

She spelled out the words slowly and precisely as if explaining to a rather slow child.

'Now what part of this do you not understand, Vincenzo?'

'All of it!' he tossed at her, a blaze of derision in his eyes, scorching over her exposed skin. 'You must know that today was the first time—the only time—I've seen David hold you or do anything at all to show his feelings? I cannot bring myself to believe that you would choose the milk-and-water relationship you have with him over the one you shared with me.'

'I never *shared* anything with you, Vincenzo! Nothing at all. We both took—neither of us gave...'

The lie caught in her throat, almost choking her, but she swallowed it down and forced herself to continue.

'And the only thing that held us together—the blazing sex—has burned itself out as fires like that always will. They don't last. They can't...'

'No!'

It came with the force of a thunderbolt, stopping her dead and leaving her shaking all over.

'I don't believe it—I won't believe it.'

Twice Amy opened her mouth to answer him, and twice her voice failed her so that a broken croak was the only sound that she could manage. She had just swallowed hard to try to ease her parched throat enough to try again when she was saved by an unexpected intervention.

'Amy?' David's voice called from the living room, a note of annoyance shading her name. 'What the devil's keeping you? How long does it take you to make a pot of tea?'

'Just coming!' Amy managed, affecting an ease she was so very far from feeling. 'I'll be there in a minute.'

A few moments of flurried movement put the teapot on the tray, the mugs, sugar and milk by its side. Picking it up, Amy turned towards the door then swung back to glare furiously into Vincenzo's dark face.

'Believe it!' she said savagely. 'Because that's how it is. How it always will be!'

And shouldering the door open she marched out of the room, her head held defiantly high.

CHAPTER ELEVEN

SHE had thought that Vincenzo might have the tact to leave her and David alone, but he followed her back into the living room, settling again in one of the armchairs.

For courtesy's sake she was forced to offer him tea, only to find that by the time she had poured it, he was deep in conversation with David about the problems of building business premises locally. He barely acknowledged her actions with a brief nod before continuing his discussion.

Cursing silently under her breath, Amy deliberately seated herself well away from him, taking a place beside David on the settee. But to her annoyance, her gesture went unnoticed; Vincenzo did not even take his eyes off the man opposite. Fuming, Amy could only sit silent and listen, her thoughts drifting until something she heard David say dragged them right back to the present.

'Tell me, Vincenzo, doesn't your wife object to your being away so long? You've been in England for three weeks now—is she likely to join you at any point?'

Amy's tea slopped over in her saucer as she sat up sharply, nerves twisting in apprehension at the thought of just what Vincenzo might reply to that. She knew her face had paled, knew that Vincenzo's dark, assessing eyes had flicked to it then away again, his attention apparently directed on David as he seemed to consider his answer.

'I'm in contact with my wife every single day,' he returned smoothly. 'So she never feels neglected. As to whether she's likely to join us, I think she's perfectly comfortable where she is. I don't expect that she'll want to move in the near future.'

In spite of herself, Amy couldn't help feeling admiration

for the way he had side-stepped David's question without ever compromising his determination never to lie. Meeting the gleaming black eyes that challenged her to object, she lifted her cup in a parody of a toast, seeing the corners of his lips twitch in amused response.

The next moment the cup clattered down into the saucer, as David turned his head towards her, narrowly missing catching sight of the gesture

'That's a pity, isn't it, Amy? It would have been nice to invite her here for your birthday.'

Amy's mind boggled at the thought and she had to struggle to compose her features into some degree of calm in order to answer him.

Vincenzo got there first.

'That's right. It's next week, isn't it? July the twenty-sixth.'

'How do you know that?'

Panic flared in Amy's mind, obliterating all rational thought. All she could picture was the moment that, in order to complete the formalities for their wedding, she had told Vincenzo her birth date. She could still visualise his smile, hear his beautiful voice say softly, 'So you're a Leo? It figures. A lioness suits you perfectly—proud and strong and deeply sensual at heart.'

Vincenzo didn't even miss a beat.

'You told me, didn't you, Amy? Some time ago.'

Carefully omitting the fact that 'some time' was over four years before. Amy felt the stretched nerves that had coiled into knots begin to untangle, only to have them tighten again as the conversation continued.

'Are you going to do anything special?'

'As a matter of fact, I've rented a cottage in the Lake District for the weekend.'

She'd planned it a couple of months ago, never suspecting then that by the time the date of her birthday came around she would view the short break not just as a couple

of days' relaxation but more as an escape from the strain
of having to watch every word she said.

She was suddenly unable to sit still and got to her feet,
crossing to replace her cup on the tray, then froze as she
heard Vincenzo's next words from behind her.

'I have never seen that part of your country. I am told
that it's very beautiful.'

The louse was blatantly angling for an invitation to join
her. Anger ripped through her, blowing a fuse in her
thoughts. Whirling round, she faced Vincenzo, just as
David opened his mouth to speak.

'No!' she flung the words furiously at Vincenzo's smiling face. 'No way at all! You're not—'

'Amy!' David's reproof cut through her outburst, shocking her into silence. 'I'm truly sorry,' he went on, addressing the other man. 'I really don't know what's come over
her. It's not like her at all.'

'No problem.'

Vincenzo's smile was calculated to mean totally different
things to both of the people present, Amy knew. To David,
it was pure man-to-man, united in the face of the irrational
behaviour of women. To Amy, however, it had another
interpretation entirely. It revealed an amused appreciation
of the fact that he believed that this *was* the real Amy,
certainly it was the one he knew only too well.

The temptation to round on him, give him a piece of her
mind, was strong. But she knew that she had shocked David
already. He would be stunned if she went any further.
Stunned and disapproving of her behaviour towards a man
he viewed as an important client. So she contented herself
with looking pointedly at her watch, silently communicating the lateness of the hour.

To her surprise, Vincenzo took the hint, getting to his
feet and stretching lazily.

'I think it's time I left you two alone,' he said, his tone
implying an indulgent understanding of the needs of a cou-

ple he believed to be lovers that set Amy's teeth strongly on edge. *'Buona notte*, David—Amy.'

It was all that Amy could do to acknowledge his departure. Her relief at seeing him leave was diluted by the fact that she fully expected that David was not going to leave things this way. He had obviously been shocked by her outburst, and clearly intended saying so.

She was right. The door had barely closed behind Vincenzo when David got to his feet and turned to her, disapproval written all over his face.

'What on earth came over you? I've never known you be as rude as that—and to a man of Signor Ravenelli's standing...'

She'd always know that David had this side to him, Amy reflected, tuning out his tirade by going deep inside her own thoughts. Always known that status and money meant more to him than it would ever do to her.

Now, knowing that Vincenzo was watching every move David made, every word he spoke, she was aware of everything in a new and very disturbing way. It was as if someone had switched on a brilliant, searching spotlight, focusing it directly on her life, and she wasn't at all sure that she was happy with the things it was revealing.

She so much wanted David to be the sort of man who would impress Vincenzo. She needed him to drive all doubts from the Italian's mind, force him to admit that here was a man he knew Amy could be happy with. Only then would he concede and sign the divorce papers.

So she had found herself unbearably sensitive to everything about her boss, seeing him through the other man's eyes. And the problem was that where before she had been able to gloss over petty, carping criticisms, or his dogmatic insistence on work being the driving force of his life, now such things stuck out like a sore thumb, impossible to ignore.

David was coming to the end of his rant—really, there

was no other word for it—and Amy hastily shook herself back into the present.

'I'll see you tomorrow. I hope you'll be in a better mood then.'

Amy fought hard with herself all the way to the door, knowing he expected her to apologise but equally aware of the way that the word sorry would stick in her throat. It was only when David's grasp was actually on the handle that she found something with which to break her uncomfortable silence.

'I really would prefer not to be alone with Vincenzo at the cottage.'

She hadn't anticipated how he might interpret that remark and was stunned when immediately all trace of annoyance and bad temper evaporated from David's face to be replaced by an indulgent smile.

'I understand now. You're thinking of a romantic weekend—just the two of us—'

'No…'

It was a squawk of protest. One that David ignored completely.

'Come here…'

Amy froze in shock and disbelief as he grabbed at her, hauling her into his arms without a care for her rigid stiffening away from him. His mouth crushed hers, hot and wet, and totally unwanted.

How could David ever have thought she wanted a romantic weekend alone with him? And she certainly hadn't given him the encouragement he seemed to assume now as he lifted a hand to cup the curve of her breast, making her jump in shock like a frightened, disturbed cat.

'David!' she protested sharply, grateful for the fact that he stilled at once in response to her sharp protest.

'What? Am I taking things a bit too fast?' He seemed totally unabashed by her obvious consternation. 'But I thought…'

'Well, you thought wrong...' Amy muttered, then hastily rethought. Whatever else he was, David was still her boss. 'I think we've got our wires crossed,' she amended awkwardly. 'Probably my fault... I'm really not feeling too brilliant tonight. I—haven't been sleeping too well lately...'

Understatement of the century! She hadn't had a decent night's sleep ever since Vincenzo had moved in. It had been impossible to relax knowing that he was only a few feet away, across the landing, that every movement she made, every creak of the bed might carry to where he lay, revealing just how restless her nights were.

'I think I need an early night—try to get some rest.'

To her relief he didn't argue.

'You do that then. I'll ring you tomorrow to see how you are.'

Giving her cheek a pat that was nothing short of paternal, he left. Amy watched him walk briskly down the garden path before she let the door swing shut and leaned back weakly against it, closing her eyes in a gesture of exhausted relief.

'So you're still not sleeping well.'

The drawling, softly accented voice broke into her reverie, snapping her head up sharply, a groan escaping her involuntarily. Of course she was not alone. She hadn't been alone for weeks now.

'Insomnia can be very distressing...'

Vincenzo straightened up from where he had been lounging against the wall at the end of the small hallway.

'I can offer you a cure for that.'

'I'm sure you can!' Amy flashed, glaring up at this intruder into her life—a dark, sleek cuckoo that had invaded her comfortable little nest and was set on destroying it totally. 'And I can just imagine exactly what is going through that filthy cesspool of a mind of yours. Well, for your information, the answer is no. No, I will not sleep with you; no, you cannot—'

'I suggest you wait until you're invited,' Vincenzo inserted silkily, wrong-footing her completely. 'I don't recall saying anything about taking you to bed. What I had in mind was a drink my *Nonna* always made me if I couldn't sleep. It's a combination of—'

'I'm sorry!'

Conscience forced her to say it; forced her to face the fact that, this time at least, she had misjudged him.

To her consternation, weak tears were pricking at her eyes and she dashed them away angrily with the back of her hand. They were the last thing she needed now. But his unexpected concern had been positively the last straw, knocking down defences that were already dangerously impaired.

'I didn't think…'

'Credit me with some standards,' Vincenzo's tone was icy. 'I promised I would wait. That I would watch you with this David and see if he could offer you happiness. I intend to keep to my word.'

'Thank you…'

It was just a whisper, a thin thread of sound that he must have had to strain to hear, but she was incapable of anything more. The truth was that she didn't know whether she wanted him to keep to his word or not.

'But that doesn't mean that I am not tempted.'

His voice changed dramatically on the last phrase, thickening, becoming raw and harsh with an unexpected emotion.

'That I don't want to take you in my arms and kiss you senseless, drive that "darling" you called him right back down your lying throat, erase the touch of his kisses from your lips and replace them with my own until all you can feel, all you can taste is me.'

'Vincenzo…'

She had never seen him like this before. Never seen that

blaze of passion in his eyes, heard the fervour that roughened his usually smooth tones.

'So tell me,' he swept on, ignoring her stumbling interjection. 'Tell me what it was like for you. How does your cold-blooded Englishman kiss you? Does he take your mouth with a hunger that makes your senses swim? Does his passion burn you right to your soul? *Tell me!*' he ordered, when she could only stare at him in blank confusion.

'It's—' She had no idea what to say. 'It's—it's nice...' she lied desperately.

'Nice!'

He made the word sound like an expletive.

'Nice! *Per Dio*, how dare you? How *dare* you even think of turning from my arms and into his? How dare you exchange what we had for this insipid apology for a relationship?'

'I...' Amy tried again but with no more success.

'Do you know how it feels? How it has been these past weeks? Well, I'll tell you. I have to stand and watch him kiss you—paw at you...'

His hands flew up in a violent expression of all the things he couldn't find the words to say, even his fluent English deserting him in the force of his emotions.

But then his mood changed again with bewildering speed, leaving her feeling as if her head was spinning as he held out his hand, long fingers beckoning to her.

'Come to me,' he commanded, low and gentle, huskily enticing, impossible to resist. 'Come to me and let me show you what a kiss could be like, how a woman should be held, how a lover should touch... Come to me, *innamorata*, and I will teach you what it means to be made love to...'

In her mind, Amy knew that refusal was the only safe option; that she should turn and run, escape while she could. But her mind wasn't strong enough to resist the tug of other, far more primitive temptations, hold out against the sensual spell of his words and his eyes and all they promised.

Vincenzo's arms had closed around her before she was fully aware that she had moved, holding her softly yet so firmly that she knew she could never break away.

And the truth was that she didn't want to. This felt so good. It was frightening how right it felt to be there, how safe. It was as if to be here, in his arms, to be held like this was what she had been born for. And yet reality was that 'safe' was the exact opposite of what she should be thinking. Emotionally, she had never been in greater danger in her life.

But then his dark head lowered and his lips took hers and instantly thinking became a total impossibility.

What stunned her was his gentleness. The delicacy she hadn't anticipated, the tenderness that made her mouth part on a sigh of sheer delight. But of course, Vincenzo knew what he was doing.

If he had been forceful and demanding, if the hunger that had blazed in his words, his eyes, had been there in his kiss, then she would have panicked and resisted, fighting hard to be free. But this was a slow, delicious seduction of the senses, a delicate enticement that gently teased and awakened each tiny nerve, making her head swim and every inch of her skin flood with heat.

'Vincenzo…'

The syllables of his name were a soft, swooning sound against his lips, the only response she was capable of forming. She was adrift on a golden sea of sensation, floating luxuriously. The sounds of the cars in the street outside, all awareness of her surrounding blurred into a burning haze. All she knew was Vincenzo and the deep, yearning need he woke inside her. Her breasts stung with sensitivity and there was a heated ache between her legs, making her crush herself closer, hard up against the potent evidence of his forceful arousal.

'Can your Englishman do this?' Vincenzo murmured against her mouth. 'Can he kiss you this way, make you feel this need, this passion? Does David tell you how beautiful you are, how... Amy?' His voice changed as he felt her involuntary reaction. 'Amy, what is it?'

He should never have spoken: the sound of the words was like a blow to her head, shattering the protective bubble that enclosed her, sealing her off from reality.

'No!' It was a moan of pain, of loss and bitter disillusionment. 'No!'

With a movement that wrenched at her heart as well as her body, she twisted her head away from his kisses, thankful that the movement also kept her from having to see his face. She didn't dare to look into those burning onyx eyes, fearful of what she might read there. His physical reaction was bad enough, the sudden total stillness terrifying, the instant withdrawal that she could sense through the way he held her making her shiver in apprehension.

'No. Stop! I won't let you do this!'

'Won't let me?' Vincenzo echoed on a dangerous note. 'Amy, *carissima*, you cannot say that. This is what we were made for, you and I. To deny it is to deny yourself—your heart—your soul.'

It came too close to her own thoughts of just seconds before, throwing her into a panic so that she snatched at the first thing that came into her mind to use as a shield against him.

'But David...'

The use of the other man's name was like a sword coming down between them, driving them apart. With a harsh, violent curse, Vincenzo let her go, releasing her so rapidly that she fell back against the wall, her hands going out to support her.

'David! David is nothing! He's all wrong for you.'

'No, he's not!' Amy bluffed wretchedly, praying he wouldn't see through her smokescreen, realise she was protesting far, far too much. 'He's what I need. He's calm, he's organised, he…'

The cynical lifting of one dark eyebrow almost destroyed her, bringing her up sharp against the way that she wasn't even sounding convincing.

'He brings me flowers.'

Her wild gesture directed that cold-eyed gaze to the vase of flowers she had been arranging earlier. Vincenzo spared the glorious display a single, scathing glance.

'He brings you *roses*,' he drawled sardonically. 'When anyone who knows you knows that they are far from your favourite flower. A lover would bring you freesias.'

'He tries,' Amy whispered struggling not to remember a time in Venice when she had opened the door to her hotel room to find the air filled with the heady perfume of vase after vase of her absolute favourite flower arranged to cover every available surface. 'He wants me to be happy.'

'Trying and wanting are not enough.'

'And neither are passion and physical desire! Passion burns, Vincenzo, it hurts…it destroys. Without love, it's like a forest fire raging out of control, or a tornado that sweeps aside everything in its path. And when it burns itself out, as it inevitably must…'

'You would still be my wife.'

'In a marriage that was a lie from start to finish.'

'I vowed to love…'

'Oh, don't bring that word into it!'

Amy's hands came up before her, as if to protect herself from the impact of the word she knew he didn't mean.

'Just because you took a vow, it doesn't mean you know how to *love*!'

'And David does? He is truly what you choose?'

For a long, silent moment the question seemed to hang in the air between them like a physical barrier, impossible to brush aside.

'I don't know,' Amy acknowledged at last, expelling the

words on a sigh of resignation. 'I only know that I don't choose you.'

Please don't let him fight me on this! she prayed as the words died away. Don't make me have to say it again, because I really don't think I could manage it.

Through dull, clouded eyes, she watched Vincenzo's proud head go back, his anger fade to a cold, bitter derision that seared over her exposed nerves in scathing contempt.

'I said you were a coward,' he drawled at last, 'but I had no idea just how craven you were. You talk of passion but you don't know what the word means.'

Slowly, he shook his head, as if in disbelief at her foolishness, then an arrogant flick of his hand seemed to dismiss her totally from his thoughts.

'Go to your David, Amy, *bella mia,*' he flung at her, the contempt in his tone eating into her soul like acid. 'Go to him and live your emotional half-life; it's what you deserve. *He's* what you deserve. But if sometimes at night the hunger comes over you—if you lie awake and think of how it might have been, then remember what you could have had, but you were too faint-hearted to take it. And perhaps, when that moment comes, you'll recognise the mistake you made and wish it could be otherwise—but by then it will be far, far too late.'

Pivoting on his heel, he turned and strode away from her without a backward glance. And Amy could only watch him go.

Just for one brief moment, the impulse to call him back almost overwhelmed her. She even opened her mouth to try, but hastily closed it again, recognising the danger she was in.

He was right, she acknowledged, sinking back against the wall, overwhelmed by a terrible desolation. In the future she would look back and remember, and regret what might have been.

But the problem was that her 'what might have been'

and the one Vincenzo was thinking of were not the same. They were at totally opposite ends of the emotional spectrum, and that was the real reason why she had been forced to make the choice she had. A choice that hadn't been a choice at all, but purely a matter of survival.

CHAPTER TWELVE

As THE car drew to a halt outside the small, white-painted cottage, Amy found it impossible not to reflect on just how different this arrival was from the one that she had been anticipating. And not just because she wasn't here on her own as she'd expected.

'Why the big sigh?' the man at her side asked. 'Are you wishing David was here with you?'

'We both know that was impossible,' she returned tartly, well aware of the fact that she was dodging the issue. 'He had to stay behind to sort out that business deal.'

'Otherwise he would be here, and I'd be the one back in Charnham,' Vincenzo drawled. 'Which is no doubt exactly where you wish I was right now.'

With an effort Amy produced a shrug that she prayed expressed total indifference to his statement.

'The cottage has two perfectly adequate bedrooms. You're welcome to the use of one of them. After all, we've managed—what is it?—over a month now of li—'

Nervously she danced away from the emotive term 'living together'.

'Of sharing accommodation in my flat. This can hardly be much more of a problem.'

Except that this cottage was even smaller than she had expected, probably taking up less space than her home. They would practically be living on top of one another and, after the stresses and strains of the past weeks, that was not a prospect she anticipated with any degree of relish.

She hadn't realised that they were going to be quite so far from civilisation, either. The postal address of the cottage might have been Grasmere, but they had driven through the village over half an hour ago, finally finding their destination at the end of a long, winding track, a mile or more from anything that could be called a road.

This must be why it had been advertised as a honeymoon cottage. It would be perfect for anyone who wanted peace and quiet and just each other's company. But the cruel irony of this trip was that it was to discuss the break-up of a marriage, not the start of one,

She still hadn't fully come to terms with the way that she had been manoeuvred into taking Vincenzo with her. She had just about decided to abandon the idea of the weekend in the Lake District, giving it up as a bad job. But then Vincenzo had started manipulating the situation.

'If you want this divorce, then there are things we need to discuss,' he'd told her. 'This weekend cottage you've booked seems like the perfect place to do that.'

'We can talk about them here!' Amy had protested, the thought of being here alone with Vincenzo tightening every muscle in rejection.

'Not without David dropping in and interfering every minute,' Vincenzo pointed out. 'If you're not at work with him, then he's here. We don't need any interruptions.'

Which was something she couldn't deny, Amy admitted privately. David just didn't seem to get the message that his attentions weren't welcomed. He'd stunned her completely by turning up with an unexpected and, for David, a surprisingly carefully chosen birthday present of her favourite perfume and a beautiful silk scarf, and no amount of hinting could stop him from almost taking up residence in her flat. In the end she had given up trying to be gentle, and had told him straight that there could never be any relationship between them.

But not before David had even tried to interfere in her arrangements for her weekend away, something that Vincenzo had coolly exploited to his own advantage when he had discussed the holiday in front of her boss. Knowing

only too well that David, with his determination to please
this most valuable customer, would support him, he had
once more spun the story of wanting to see the Lake
District until David took up his cause.

'Don't be a silly girl...'

David covered her hand with his, setting her teeth on
edge.

'You go ahead and enjoy the break. You deserve it.
Leave me to sort out this Ravenhead deal and you show
Vincenzo some of the beauties of our countryside.'

'I don't think...'

Despairingly, Amy swung round to where Vincenzo
stood, silently watching and listening. In spite of herself,
she couldn't resist searching his face, hoping against hope
that she would find something there that would give her a
clue to work on, a chance of changing his mind.

But the expression etched on to those stunning features,
gleaming in the polished jet eyes, was one that twisted her
nerves in fear, telling her without words that there was no
way she could win.

You wouldn't dare, that look challenged silently. You
wouldn't dare invite me to go along with you. You're
scared. And if you're scared, then that means something
else. It means that this matters more to you than you're
prepared to admit. That you feel something more than
you've been pretending all this time. If you're so afraid of
my company, then it means that you *care*.

Silently Amy admitted defeat. There was nothing else
she could do. To protest would only be to reinforce his
conviction that she was afraid of him.

The only way she could refute that assumption was to
smile as light-heartedly as she could manage.

And say, 'Yes, okay. Why not?'

'Better get inside,' Vincenzo warned now, coming past
her with the bags as she stood outside the cottage. 'Looks
like it's going to rain.'

Sure enough, with the typical changeability of an English summer, the clear, bright afternoon was rapidly clouding over, a chill wind getting up, pushing Amy into hurrying after him. The first heavy drops of rain began to fall just as she stumbled into the small, narrow hall.

Vincenzo was standing at the foot of the stairs, tall and dark in a navy V-necked sweatshirt and jeans. Meeting his deep eyes in a moment of intense awareness, Amy felt her heartbeat quickening, her breathing suddenly uneven. It was almost as if she had suddenly come up against a dark, sleek predator, waiting and watching for its prey.

'I'll take the bags up.'

His voice was calm, indifferent. Was she the only one who had felt that stunning jolt of recognition, the feeling of being on very dangerous ground indeed?

'Any particular choice in rooms?'

'What? No…'

Amy gave a swift glance up the narrow, steep stairs. If anything, the landing was smaller than the hallway. She would be able to hear every move he made at night, every slight sound—and vice versa. The thought made her voice wobble as she went on, 'Anywhere will do. It's just somewhere to sleep.'

Something in her tone had got through to him, making him pause and look deep into her eyes.

'David could have been here if he'd wanted to be,' he said abruptly.

'Don't be silly.' The fear of betraying the truth made her tone sharper than she'd intended. 'He had an important contract to deal with—something that could bring in a lot of money.'

'Exactly,' Vincenzo returned cryptically.

He was turning away as he spoke, heading up the stairs.

'Vincenzo!'

His response was so swift, so automatic, dropping the

cases and swinging back to face her, that it seemed he had been anticipating her call.

'*Si?*'

'Why—why are you here?'

'I thought you understood. To talk about the divorce.'

'And that's all?'

Even to herself she couldn't have said if she was relieved or disappointed by his answer.

'All?' he echoed sombrely. 'No, but you wouldn't want to know about the rest.'

'And what "rest" is that?'

His smile was slow, strangely gentle.

'Oh, Amy, *cara*, I think you already know the answer to that. I am here because I cannot be anywhere else. Because, no matter how hard I try, I cannot stay away.'

'But you said… I thought…'

Since that night he had kissed her at her flat, he had never said another word about wanting her. Foolishly, naïvely, she had allowed herself to believe it was all over. That he had conceded defeat, or at the very least decided she wasn't worth fighting for. She should have known better. Conceding defeat and Vincenzo Ravenelli were two things that just didn't go together.

'Believe me, *bella mia*, I don't like it any more than you do, but you have a hold on me that I cannot break. So…' He spread his hands, palms upwards in a gesture of something like acceptance. 'I am here…'

The tension Amy was already experiencing was multiplied one hundred fold in an instant.

'You needn't think…' she began nervously, only to have the word fade from her mind when she was confronted by another of those slow smiles.

'Don't worry, *moglie mia*, I am not a complete fool. I do not put my head in a noose twice. I told you, I will not come to you again. If you want me, you will have to come to me.'

'I'd rather crawl all the way home over broken glass! If that's what you're waiting for, *marito mio*...' Deliberately she echoed his tone of voice. 'Then you'll have to wait until that lake out there freezes over!'

'Really?'

Vincenzo cocked his head on one side, listening to the rain that was now lashing against the windows, the gale that howled round the cottage.

'Seems to me that that might not be as distant a prospect as you might think,' he tossed at her before heading back upstairs with the cases, leaving Amy gasping in fury behind him.

Did he really think, even now, that she would change her mind, beg him to come back to her? The arrogance of the man! She would...

No! Amy pulled herself up sharply. Getting angry, getting upset was exactly what Vincenzo wanted. Well, she'd show him!

'I thought we'd take it in turns to cook,' she purred, all sweetness and light, when Vincenzo came back downstairs again. 'I'll do tonight, and it'll be your turn tomorrow. That okay?'

'Fine.' Just for a second he had looked taken aback by her quick recovery, but it only took a second for him to match her in casual politeness. 'Shall I light a fire? This place doesn't have any central heating and the rain's really brought the temperature down.'

This was going to be easy, Amy told herself as she bustled about the kitchen preparing the meal. All she had to do was keep the conversation neutral and she'd be fine. It was just like going on holiday with a friend.

Okay, she admitted a short time later, so if Vincenzo was a *friend*, then her pulse wouldn't leap quite so frantically when he brushed past her in the tiny kitchen. She wouldn't be so sensually aware of little things about him, like the strength implied by the easy way he carried in a huge basket of logs from the outside store, the strong lines of his hands as he laid the fire, the strangely vulnerable look of the back of his neck between the silky black hair and the soft navy sweatshirt. But she wasn't going to act on that, so she was quite safe.

Her resolve got her through that first evening, and most of the next day. A day when the rain hardly let up at all and yet Vincenzo insisted on them going out, on seeing everything they could cram into a day.

'I showed you Venice,' he said. 'It's your turn now.'

'But we're not here to go sightseeing. I thought you wanted to discuss the—the divorce.'

Her voice shook on the last couple of words as she struggled to accept that this was really going to happen. After wanting it for so long, forcing herself to go along with Vincenzo's conditions, she couldn't believe that she was so close to winning her freedom. It ought to make her feel happier, lighter, as if a burden had dropped from her shoulders, but instead her mood was low and despondent, grey and dull as the weather.

'We have the whole weekend for that, and right now you're so painfully uptight that you wouldn't be able to talk straight if you tried.'

In spite of herself Amy blinked in confusion at his pronouncement. She had thought she'd played the role of careless about-to-be-divorcee to perfection so it was disturbing to know that Vincenzo had seen straight through her act and discovered the truth underneath it.

'We can talk tonight. Today we explore the area.'

'What? In this? You must be mad!'

'Are you afraid of a little rain, Amy? We won't melt.'

'No, but we might well drown! Oh, all right.' Shaking her head in disbelief, she pulled her coat from the hook behind the door. 'Come on, then—let's do the guided tour.'

In spite of, or perhaps because of the weather, she ended up enjoying herself. There was a special sort of community atmosphere that had sprung up because of the torrential downpour. People laughed and grimaced and commented on the weather as they trudged round the narrow streets of Grasmere, dodging in and out of shops simply in order to get a respite from being soaked.

It was the same in Keswick where they found a small restaurant and lingered as long as possible over lunch, only risking coming out when a faint crack appeared in the clouds, a tempting sliver of blue sky showing through the grey.

It didn't last. After no more than ten minutes, the weather closed in again, the rain heavier than before, but by that time Amy was past caring, the absurdity of sightseeing in such appalling weather appealing to her sense of the ridiculous and lightening her mood.

'I can't get any more wet than I already am!' she laughed, surveying the sodden bottoms of her jeans, her rain-darkened shoes. 'I'm just going to ignore it.' And she did her Gene Kelly impression, dancing along the street, humming 'Singing in the Rain' as she did so.

'You're mad!' Now Vincenzo was the one who hunched his shoulders against the showers. 'Totally out of your mind.'

'I'm English!' Amy retorted. 'And we English were born to handle the rain. I reckon we're part ducks, really. You didn't know I had webbed feet inside these boots, did you? Oh, darn it…'

She screwed up her face into a grimace of discomfort as a particularly large raindrop splashed from an overhead awning, bounced on her head and trickled down her nose.

'Here…'

Reaching into his pocket, Vincenzo pulled out a spotless white handkerchief and dabbed at her nose, drying it gently.

'Thank—' Amy began then froze, staring straight into his face.

It really wasn't fair, she told herself regretfully. Where

she knew that she must look like a particularly miserable drowned rat, all that the rain had done was to enhance Vincenzo's own particular brand of lethal male attractiveness.

Soaking wet, the black hair looked smooth and sleek, pressed down flat against the superb bone structure of his skull, and emphasising the slashing lines of his cheekbones, the straight nose and determined jaw. The rain had caught in the impossibly long, lush lashes that fringed his spectacular eyes, clumping them into spikes through which the polished jet gleamed, warmed by soft amusement.

But even as she watched the amusement faded, to be replaced by something deeper, infinitely more disturbing. The soft pad of the handkerchief stilled, Vincenzo abandoning all pretence at drying her face.

'Amy…' he began with a hesitancy that was so unlike Vincenzo that she had to blink hard to convince herself she wasn't hearing things.

But in that same moment there was a huge flash of lightning, a crash of thunder almost overhead, and the intensity of the storm increased by a thousand per cent.

'Oh, no!'

Snapped out of the strange, hypnotic mood, Amy jumped, looking round frantically.

'Over there—' She grabbed Vincenzo's arm and pointed. 'There's a bookshop—we can hide in it till this passes.'

In the flurry and haste of the mad dash across the road, dodging pedestrians, puddles, and traffic, the atmosphere was broken. When she had the nerve to look into Vincenzo's face again, his mood was obviously completely different. He turned his attention to the bookshelves as if nothing had happened, and the moment of distraction was never referred to again.

In the beginning, the second evening of the holiday followed the pattern of the first. The first necessity when they arrived back at the cottage was a hot shower and a complete change of clothes. They were both soaked through to the skin and ravenously hungry, so dinner was the next item on the agenda. Amy devoured the savoury pasta dish Vincenzo had created with appetite and enjoyment.

'That was great!' she told him, genuinely enthusiastic, as she pushed her plate away from her and leaned back in her chair. 'You really can cook, can't you?'

'Don't look so surprised.' Vincenzo assumed an expression of mock outrage. 'Of course I can cook! I am Italian, after all.'

'Well, I'm impressed. One day you'll make someone a wonderful wife.'

Her words fell into a sudden silence, everything left unsaid about the true reason they were there seeming to hover between them like a great black shadow, destroying the light mood in the space of a heartbeat. Immediately, Amy wished them back, but it was too late for that, so she got hastily to her feet, desperate to change the subject.

'I'll do the washing up.'

'No need...' Vincenzo was on his feet too, collecting plates from the table. 'I'll do it.'

'But you cooked!' Amy protested. 'It's only fair.'

In the end they did it together, a situation that started off relaxed and ended up with Amy's nerves stretched to screaming point. The kitchen really was far too small for comfort, the confined space forcing them close to each other time and time again. And the whole situation was just too cosily domestic. Anyone looking through the lighted window from outside would have taken them for a long-married couple, perfectly in tune with each other and the ironic contrast between that scenario and the truth about their painfully short marriage twisted a knife in her heart.

So it was a relief when the simple task was over and she could escape upstairs to draw breath and collect the fat novel she had bought in Keswick as they sheltered from the rain. Curling up in an elderly armchair beside the fire, she concentrated fiercely on the plot so as to block out the faint noises Vincenzo made as he pottered about in the kitchen.

Outside, the rain, which had slowed to just a drizzle while they ate, had begun to fall in torrents again, and in the distance the roar of thunder blended in with the sigh of the wind.

'Coffee?' Vincenzo asked, coming to the door.

'Mmm, that'd be nice.'

Amy turned a page one-handed, using the other to tuck away a strand of hair that, slippery smooth after its dowsing in the rain, had fallen forwards onto her face. It fell down again immediately, and again the next time she tucked it back.

With a small sound of impatience she reached up, pulled out the band that fastened her hair back into its usual chignon so that it fell loose around her shoulder and combed through with her fingers. She was just about to scrape it back again when a sound from the door made her pause.

'Leave it down.' Vincenzo's voice was soft and husky.

'What?'

Looking up, she found that her gaze met his, locked and held, unable to look away again.

'I said, leave it down. It looks better that way.'

'I…'

She was tempted. It was much more comfortable and relaxed that way. And there was a look in Vincent's eyes, a warmth that was like a caress in itself, that she both longed to keep there, and yet at the same time feared the consequences if she encouraged him.

'And David isn't here to disapprove.'

'He doesn't… Oh, dear…'

Suddenly she was desperately tired of defending David, of trying to explain everything he did.

'He is a bit old-fashioned.'

Tell him now, her conscience urged. Tell him the truth

about you and David. Tell him how, only the day before, you spelled out in no uncertain terms to David, the fact that there could never be anything other than friendship between the two of you. But the words tied themselves into a knot in her throat and she couldn't get them to form into actual sounds.

'I think that's an understatement,' Vincenzo murmured dryly. 'Don't tell me he approved of that top.'

'This?'

Amy looked down in consternation at the rich teal velvet of her loose, long-sleeved top. She had seen it in a shop only the day before, and had been unable to resist it, even though she had wondered then exactly when she might get the chance to wear it. In the rush to get dry and the amicable dispute over who should have the shower first, she hadn't even stopped to think but had grabbed the first thing that came to hand.

'No.' It was a faint sigh. 'It's not exactly David's sort of thing. I don't suppose he'd be too impressed by this, either...' She smoothed a hand over the black jersey of her ankle-length skirt.

'I like it,' Vincenzo told her softly. 'Sitting there by the fire, it makes you look like someone in a Victorian painting. But David will never know. He's far too busy negotiating terms for the Ravenshead contract to even spare a thought for what we're doing.'

It was the way he pronounced the name Ravenshead that gave him away. Any English person would have made it sound like the name of the bird, but Vincenzo's accent, his intonation meant that it echoed his own surname, bring her head up sharply.

'Raven...' she began, struggling to cope with the thoughts that were crowding into her head, the implications for herself if her suspicions were true. 'Ravenshead—Ravenelli! It's another of your companies—it's your damn contract!'

At least he had the grace not to try and deny it. She wouldn't have believed him if he had. The truth had been written on his face in the moment she had accused him.

'Just why are you putting all this work David's way? It can't be just altruism—making sure his company doesn't go under.'

'It's definitely not that. I'm not a fool, Amy. I've seen the work Brooke's does, and it's good—they deserve the contract. But I have to admit to another, more personal motive for what I've been doing.'

'And that is?' Amy questioned, not really knowing whether she wanted the answer. Her heartbeat had suddenly picked up a gear, sending the blood pulsing through her veins so that it roared in her ears until she had to strain to hear.

'I wanted to make sure that David wouldn't be here. That he wouldn't suddenly decide to join us. It didn't take much doing. All I had to do was to dangle a nice fat contract under his nose and he forgot all about the needs of the woman he is supposed to want to marry.'

'You...' Amy could not believe what she was hearing. 'But *why*?'

Vincenzo's eyes were just deep, black pools, holding her gaze, drawing her in.

'Isn't it obvious?' he murmured, his voice deepening by an octave or more. 'I wanted to be alone with you.'

'To discuss the divorce—yes, I know that.'

'I doubt if you do,' Vincenzo returned huskily, black eyes fixed on her face. 'You must know that the divorce was only an excuse.'

'An...You...' Amy began, but the crash of thunder directly overhead drowned out her words.

It was followed almost immediately by a brilliant flash of lighting that flared through the room, illuminating it brilliantly. That had barely died away, in fact Amy was still blinking hard in shock, when all the lights in the cottage flickered for a moment and then went out, leaving them completely in the dark.

CHAPTER THIRTEEN

'CENZO!'

Amy was too shocked, too off-balance mentally to realise that she had used the old, affectionate form of his name.

'It's okay, *cara*.' In contrast, Vincenzo was perfectly calm, totally in control. 'No need to panic. It looks like the storm's brought a power line down somewhere. If you just wait a moment…'

He disappeared into the kitchen, reappearing a short time later with a handful of candles.

'I saw these in one of the cupboards earlier. They should help make things easier.'

By now Amy's eyes had adjusted to the darkness and she watched him, a tall, dark shape in the shadows, as he busied himself setting the candles on saucers and in jam jars. In a couple of moments room was transformed into something resembling a fairyland with a soft, swaying light burning on every available surface.

'So what do we do now?'

'We'll have to wait until someone manages to repair it. I expect they'll get around to it sooner or later.' He sounded totally unperturbed. 'I'm afraid it won't be light enough for you to continue reading, and we'll have to forget about the coffee. But I did buy a bottle of wine today. Would you like to share that?'

'Okay.' Amy nodded.

'Then at least we can sit beside the fire and keep warm—and talk.'

Talk. Just a few moments ago she would have assumed that he meant he wanted to discuss the details of the divorce, but remembering now just what he had said in the moment before the lights had gone out, Amy could no longer be so sure. Doubt and confusion brought up her defences fast, driving her to take several steps backwards in the conversation so as to be able to glare at him as he came back in from the kitchen again, wine bottle and two glasses in one hand.

'I think the talking you have to do should be some explaining. Like just what gives you the right to interfere in my life this way, moving in and arranging things as if I were a piece on a chessboard '

'Hardly that...'

Vincenzo's attention was concentrated on the wine bottle, removing the cork with neat efficiency and pouring a couple of generous glassfuls.

'I simply arranged for David to have a choice. It was up to him what he did with it.'

'And I'm supposed to believe that if he'd told the Ravenshead representatives to go to hell, that he had other things to do, that you wouldn't have had some other card up your sleeve ready to meet just that situation?'

'What do you think?' The question came softly, tinged with a shadow that sounded strangely like regret. 'But then that problem didn't arise, did it? Because David didn't hesitate, did he? He didn't tell anyone to go to hell—except you, the woman whose feelings he should have put first, before anything else.'

'Oh!'

Amy's legs seemed unable to support her, and she sat down suddenly, landing on the thick rag rug before the fire with something of a bump. There had been such an intensity in his tone that it shook her rigid, almost making her wonder if she was still speaking to the same man.

'Here...'

Vincenzo held out a glass of wine to her, the clear, light liquid sparkling like diamonds in the flickering candle flames.

As she took it and cradled it in her hands, curling her fingers round the cool, hard glass, he came down on the rug beside her, arranging his long legs comfortably with the lazy elegance of a relaxed cat.

'Why do you do it, Amy?'

His tone had sharpened now, bringing her head up to meet the probing force of his deep set eyes. The dancing flames of the fire, yellow and gold, were reflected perfectly in their black depths, holding her fascinated.

'Why do you let him treat you like this? When you're together he shows you no special warmth, no affection. Why don't you find someone else?'

'Someone else!'

Anger flared in Amy's mind at the thought that he would argue for this someone else, when the one person she had truly wanted to treat that way, the one she wanted to show her that 'special warmth' was himself. Pushing away any thought of common sense or restraint, she took a swift swallow of her wine before setting the glass down on the hearth with a distinct crash.

'Why don't I find someone else?' she echoed in cynical mockery that didn't quite hide the pain underneath. 'Who do you suggest, Vincenzo? Someone who truly cares? Someone who sees me just as a way to get something he *really* wants? Someone who'll date me, seduce me—marry me—for nothing more than a bet?'

'It wasn't like that…' Vincenzo broke in furiously, but, launched on a sea of bitter memories, Amy couldn't stop, couldn't even think of holding back.

'Or perhaps someone who never wanted me in the first place. Someone who always saw me as a mistake, who wished I'd never been born, who—'

'*Per Dio*, Amy!' Vincenzo's raw exclamation broke into her tirade. 'What—who are you talking about?'

'My—my father…'

Stunned by the catch in his voice, the blaze of something

in his eyes that now had nothing to do with the light of the fire, Amy reached for her wine glass again, lifting it to her lips with a hand that shook perceptibly, swallowing down an unthinking amount.

'He told my mother he never wanted children. When she found out she was pregnant with me, he even considered an abortion, but she refused…'

She didn't know if it was the effect of the wine, or the darkness, the candlelight that created an unreal, private world that enclosed them completely, but suddenly the whole story was pouring out of her, her tongue tangling over the words in her haste to get them out.

She told him of the shock of her father's early death, the funeral, the appearance of the other woman and her daughters. Amy's father's children.

'She—she had two children, one the same age as me, one younger. She said that they'd always been the light of my father's life so—so *wanted*!'

Her voice broke on the final word, clashing with Vincenzo's violent curse, an outpouring of vicious Italian. She never saw him move but suddenly he was beside her, gathering her up in his arms and holding her close, tenderly wiping the tearstains from her face, smoothing back her hair.

'Why did you not tell me this before? Why did you…'

'It's hardly the sort of thing you blurt out at a first meeting, is it?' Somehow she managed a brittle laugh, one that cracked painfully in the middle. 'Hello, I'm Amy Redman. My father wished I'd never been born.'

She was about to reach for her wine again but then hastily reconsidered. She was already feeling the effects of the drink she'd had, her skin tingling, a sense of unreality creeping over her. Remembering what had happened that night in Venice, the erotic after-effects of one too many *Bellini* cocktails, she decided that control was definitely a better idea.

'I'm really good at choosing men, aren't I?' She sniffed inelegantly. 'I couldn't exactly choose my Dad—but you, and David—a guy who doesn't even know what flowers I like. Though I have to admit that he surprised me on my birthday.'

'It would have been a bigger surprise if he'd gone with what he originally planned to buy you.'

Misinterpreting the look of astonishment she turned on him, he went on, 'You'd have *wanted* an electric food processor? Amy, you don't even like cooking—you only do it when you have to—and—'

'Hang on a minute!'

Twisting round on the rug, Amy stared up into the strong boned face above her, watching the changing shape of the shadows on it as they moved and shifted with the flicker of the flames.

'How do you know what David was going to buy me for my birthday?'

She'd never actually seen Vincenzo disconcerted before and it was like a blow to her chest, making her breath catch painfully. Just for a second the dark gaze wavered, slid away to stare into the depths of the fire.

'He discussed it with you! He…' Another realisation followed hard on the first, leaving her punch drunk, shaking her head in bemusement. 'He told you what he was going to buy—so the perfume, the scarf… *You* suggested them!'

Vincenzo had recovered himself.

'The guy needed some help,' he drawled flippantly. 'As a lover, he hasn't even left the starting block. Would you have rather I'd let him get you that damn food processor?'

But Amy was thinking back, remembering all the other changes in David—the flowers—the dinner invitation— the kiss… Changes that had happened since Vincenzo had come to England.

'And did you encourage him to buy me flowers too? T—to…'

Had Vincenzo's 'help' been behind the way David had pounced on her? That kiss?

'What else did you suggest he should do?'

She recoiled from him in shock, her brain spinning sickeningly as she whirled from one thought to another. Why would Vincenzo, who she had believed had come to England to try and prevent a divorce, actually make an effort to *help* and encourage the man he thought of as a rival for her hand?

'He asked me what I would do if I was involved with a woman like you—how I'd behave, how I'd treat you. So I told him.'

'And, of course, you always tell the truth.'

Amy's blood was running cold in her veins, making her shiver and shift closer to the fire. She suddenly felt like the most deluded, pathetic fool in the whole of the world—totally, brilliantly deceived—and she'd never even seen it coming.

She had truly believed that when Vincenzo had said that he didn't want a divorce, that he had meant it. She had thought that she would have to struggle to win her freedom, that if he could have stopped her, he would. She couldn't have been more wrong.

The truth was that he had *wanted* to be rid of her as much as she had wanted to be free of him. And to that end he had followed her to England, not to put a spoke in what he believed was her hope of marrying David, but to make sure it happened. He had set out to turn David into a better suitor, giving him lessons in courtship, dropping hints about the things that would please her.

Because he wanted to make sure that the marriage went ahead.

He had wanted to push her into marrying David so that he would be absolutely certain he would be rid of her forever and she would never trouble him again.

And it was only as she let those words sink deep down

into her soul, gouging and stabbing all the way, that she realised quite why they hurt so much.

'What was the idea, Vincenzo?' she said, because she had to say something. It was either that or dissolve into a pathetic, shrivelled heap of misery right there in front of him.

But she still had some pride left, even if he'd just taken it and ripped it to shreds, tossing them aside with supreme indifference to what she was feeling.

'Was it that if I married David then you'd be able to skimp on the divorce settlement, maybe not pay out quite so much?'

She took a grim satisfaction in seeing the way his handsome head went back, the way the long fingers tightened around the stem of his wineglass until the knuckles showed white.

'What the...? Amy, where the devil has this come from?'

'From the devil is about right! I mean, you and he must be pretty good friends, so he gives you all his best ideas—his most cruel ones. Why else would you try and teach the man who's interested in your wife how to win her? Why—'

'Perhaps because I like a challenge?' Vincenzo inserted, stopping her dead. 'Because I don't like to win by default.'

'By...' She was completely out of her depth now.

'Amy...'

Leaning forwards, Vincenzo put down his glass and took hold of her hands instead, holding them in both of his, cupping their backs, the pad of his thumb resting in the softness of her palms.

'If David was the man you wanted, at least you deserved to have someone who was rather more what you needed than that oaf. So when he asked, I gave him a few ideas. I thought it might make you happy.'

Again that dark gaze flicked to the fire and back again, and the smile he turned on was wry and self-derisory.

'But again I have to admit to an ulterior motive.'

Now they were coming to it. Amy stirred uncomfortably, sure she didn't want to hear this, but Vincenzo held her still, tightening his grip on her hands very slightly.

'I believed that if David gave you more of the *things* you wanted and enjoy, if he behaved more like a lover—the sort of lover I believed you wanted—then you would see that it wasn't enough.'

'Enough?'

Amy was struggling to understand. And Vincenzo wasn't exactly helping because the heat of his burning gaze was scorching her skin, making her feel as if her blood was flowing hot as molten lava along her veins. And where he held her hands his thumbs were moving in slow, softly erotic circles, distracting her attention from what he was saying.

'I thought you might realise that it wasn't just the wealth that I could offer you...'

'Oh, that!' She couldn't hold back, couldn't let him go on believing that she really was capable of being so mercenary. 'That was never the case! I lied. I never wanted your money, I just wanted to feel special to someone.'

'Do you think I don't know that? Oh, I may have believed your claims that you married me for my money—at first. I may even have accused you of being a gold-digger and more. But deep down inside I knew it wasn't true. Why do you think I came after you in the first place? If you'd wanted money, you'd have taken the allowance I gave you and asked for more. But instead you tossed it right back in my face.'

His words lifted Amy's heart, gave her the confidence to speak again.

'There's something I have to ask you,' she said impulsively. 'The ring—the ruby—what did you do with it? Where is it now?'

'In a bank vault, locked away.'

The question had been a terrible mistake. She could see his instant withdrawal, the tension that tightened all the muscles in his strong jaw, the grim twist to his mouth.

'Where it can stay till the end of the world, as far as I'm concerned.'

'It means so little to you?'

He'd put her through so much, taken her heart, her body, her love and shattered them, for this—for something he simply wanted to *possess*, not even to enjoy. He had won the ring and then locked it away. He never even looked at it!

'I told you—in the end it wasn't worth it. Amy, that bet wasn't about *you*. It didn't give me what I wanted. I should never...'

'Never have married me,' Amy supplied for him, her voice cracking on the words. 'No, you shouldn't. Sal was right, you know—there was no need to take it that far. You didn't have to sign your life away.'

'No, I didn't have to do that.'

It was impossible to read his voice, his expression. The wine must have gone straight to her head because her brain definitely felt fuzzy and out of focus. Unlike her senses, which were wildly alive and buzzing with tingling sensation. And yet at the same time her heart, which had been beating far too fast, had now slowed to a heavy, languorous beat, one that echoed the heated pulse lower down in her body. And all the time his thumbs continued to stroke her hands, softly, gently, tracing small erotic patterns on her skin, sending electrical sparks of hunger fizzing through every nerve.

'I didn't have to—but you wouldn't let me touch you any other way. I understand why, now, but...'

'I would now.'

Vincenzo froze, the caress of his hands still, his eyes locking with hers so that she could be aware of nothing else.

'What did you say?'

'I would now.'

Amy couldn't believe she actually said it. Not once, but twice. The wine and Vincenzo's closeness, his touch on her skin, must have got to her tongue now, making her blurt out the secret innermost thoughts that she had been trying to hide from him all day.

No, it had nothing to do with the wine. She hadn't drunk enough for that. It was Vincenzo alone who had affected her this way. She was intoxicated, high on the sight and sound of him, the scent of his skin, the memory of his lips on hers.

'Or perhaps I mean I wouldn't—I wouldn't need marriage or even the promise of it. I wouldn't need anything.'

Absolutely still, Vincenzo drew in a deep, ragged breath and let it out again on a sigh.

'Are you saying what I think? Because if you are, you have to make it totally clear. I want there to be no mistake.'

Amy's heart clenched in momentary panic. All the complicated feelings she was struggling with seemed to have tied themselves in a knot in her throat so that she had to swallow hard to relieve the constriction.

'Do I really have to say this?' she managed.

Vincenzo's smile was slow, gentle, but it was clear he was not going to let her off the hook.

'I'm afraid you do, *carissima*. I want to hear from your own lips.'

Leaning forwards, he kissed her softly and the sensations the caress awoke in her told their own story. She no longer cared about the divorce or any part of the past. Al she wanted was Vincenzo. All she had ever needed was right here in the room with her.

'Then…'

As he had only moments before, she drew in a long, calming breath. But when she looked deep into his eyes again she was suddenly totally sure, totally strong. There was no trace of hesitation in her voice when she spoke again.

'I want you, Vincenzo. I want you to make love to me. I want it more than anything else in the world.''

'Amy...' Her name was a sigh of pure delight. 'Then come to me. Come to me, *moglie mia*, and let me kiss you.'

That bit was easy. All she had to do was to lean forwards, helped by the pull of his hands on hers, until she was half kneeling, half lying in his arms, with her head against his chest, hearing the heavy pounding beat of his heart. At last he released his grip on her fingers and one strong hand slid under her chin, lifting her face to his.

His kiss was slow and sure and infinitely tender, rousing a heat in her blood that had nothing to do with the fire at her back. Her head was swimming, her thoughts incoherent, drunk on something that was far more potent than the strongest, heady spirit. But deep inside there was one thing that she knew with absolute clarity, no room for any trace of doubt.

This was the man for her. The only man. He always had been, and he always would be. She had loved him from the moment she had first seen him and she would love him that way for the rest of her life.

And that knowledge softened her mouth under his, letting his tongue taste her fully. It relaxed her body so that he could easily take her with him down onto the rug, warmed by the firelight on one side, by the gleam of the candles at the other.

But the real heat was deep down, a molten pool of need between her thighs, one that had her stirring restlessly, a faint moan of impatience escaping her.

'Hush, *carissima*,' Vincenzo whispered softly. 'Let's take this easy. We have all the time in the world.'

And his hands were as gentle as his words as they unbuttoned the velvet top and slid it from her, smoothing and caressing the delicate skin he exposed in a way that made her arch and purr like a contented cat. Lying bathed in golden light, she submitted to the trail of kisses down her throat with a sense of such awe-filled delight that it brought a rush of tears to her eyes, seeping out from under her closed lids.

Vincenzo kissed them away so softly that she thought her heart would break at his touch.

'No tears, *innamorata*,' he murmured against her skin. 'This is not the time for them.'

'It's just…'

She couldn't complete the sentence but she had the feeling that Vincenzo didn't need her to. That he understood completely all that was in her mind and her heart, and that tears were the only way she could express it.

The rest of her clothes were eased from her so softly that she barely felt them go, only becoming aware of the fact that Vincenzo too had tossed aside his clothing when he came down beside her and she felt the heated brush of skin against skin. Hungrily she reached for him, wanting that intimate contact, needing to feel his body covering hers, her legs parting automatically, to allow him to lie between them.

'It has been so long—too long…'

Passionate desire thickened Vincenzo's accent, making it sound so much richer, more exotic than ever before, need putting a raw edge on the husky tones. His dark eyes searched her face with a laser-like intensity, watching every tiny flicker of emotion, every shift of mood, so that she knew she could hide nothing from him.

'But I have forgotten nothing. I remember every moment of the past and I still recall what you like.'

A tiny, wicked smile curled the corners of his sensually softened mouth.

'So I know that if I do this…'

His strong hands curved over her breasts, long fingers

stroking softly, tracing out delicately enticing circles of sensation.

'You will close your eyes. And if I do this…'

He moved his thumbs to rest against her nipples, teasing, tormenting, making them harden into yearning peaks of hunger.

'You will make those soft little moaning sounds that drive me wild. But if I do this…'

His dark head bent and she felt the heat of his mouth at her breast, no longer gentle but hard and demanding, driving her into a fury of longing so that her hands closed over the powerful shoulders, fingers digging into the taut muscles of his back.

'Cenzo! Oh, Cenzo!' she sighed and felt against her breast the curve of his smile that told her he had anticipated just such a reaction all along.

And in that moment it all came rushing back to her too, driving away any last traces of doubt or restraint. This was her husband, and although she had only spent that one night in his bed, she had learned a little of how to please him, too.

And so she let her fingers wander where they would, stroking, kneading, tantalising. She pressed her mouth to his shoulders, to his chest, to the flat nubs of his male nipples that hardened delightfully under the caress of her tongue. She relished the taste of him in her mouth, the feel of his hot satin skin under her wandering fingertips, the clench of tight muscles in a response he was incapable of hiding.

But in the moment that one long, muscular thigh pushed between hers to allow him access to the very heart of her femininity, she knew there was one last thing she had to say so that there could be no misunderstanding between them.

'Cenzo,' she whispered, her voice ragged with the effort it took to control herself enough to speak. 'There's something you have to know—I—I never slept with David. There's been no one...'

The admission broke off on a wild cry of response as his hand slid to the aching centre of her need, touching her lightly, making her writhe beneath him.

'I know.' His response was hoarse, shaken, betraying how close he was to losing control himself. 'I have eyes. I can see. And it's been the same for me, too. I have hungered for you, dreamed of you for four long years, and now I can't wait any longer.'

'I don't want you to,' Amy whispered against his ear, her head arching back, her whole body opening up to him, mutely inviting the heated invasion she so longed for.

'Carissima!'

It was a choked cry of delight, of triumph, of release all blended into one as he eased himself deep inside her, the glaze of passion sheening his eyes and a flare of wild colour highlighting his cheekbones as he watched her writhe in response beneath him.

'This is how it should have been, that night in Venice,' he told her, still fighting for control, his breathing ragged and rough. 'That night, I wanted you so much, I ached with hunger. This is what you owe me, *moglie mia*, what should have been mine all along...'

But Amy wasn't listening. She didn't want him to speak; she wanted him to love her. And so she moved again, circling her hips, bringing her legs up to encircle his lean hips, taking tiny, teasing little bites at his skin until, with a raw cry of surrender he gave himself up to the passion that possessed him.

And Amy too could no longer think but only feel. She was aware of nothing beyond the pulsing strength of him inside her, the soaring response he was drawing from her. Wildly, fiercely, the rhythm built, stronger and stronger, taking them both out of reality and into a place where there was no time or space, only the white heat of the final conflagration as it took them over, burning them up completely.

Afterwards, she curled up in his arms, unable to speak, incapable even of thought. And when he reached for her again, impossibly soon, she found that her responses were even quicker this time, her hunger hotter, her need greater, so that in the moment of climax she actually felt that she would shatter, splinter into fragments of delight.

At some point during the long night, when the fire had burned down low in the grate, and the candles were guttering in their holders, Vincenzo extinguished them, then lifted her and carried her to his bed. The shock of the cool sheets against her skin woke her so that she turned to him, seeking him blindly. This time their lovemaking was slower, each long drawn out second such intense delight that it brought back the tears she had known earlier.

And those tears still lingered in the exhausted aftermath, trickling down her cheeks as she lay with her head pillowed on Vincenzo's chest. They must have fallen onto his skin too because she felt him stir and look down at her.

'Tears, *carissima*?' he questioned softly. 'Why...'

Because I know how much I love you was the honest answer, but her nerve failed her, stilling the words on her tongue. But she had to say something.

'Because I could never marry anyone after this,' she managed, meaning to take it further, explain...

But heavy drugging waves of sleep washed over her before she could finish and, too worn out to fight, she gave herself up to them, knowing it didn't matter.

Vincenzo had said they had all the time in the world. Tomorrow was another day. Tomorrow they could talk. Their marriage could begin again, and this time there would be nothing to intrude on their idyll, twisting things, destroying things. That sort of malign lightning couldn't strike twice. Fate couldn't possibly be so cruel.

CHAPTER FOURTEEN

AMY'S certainty that Fate had finally decided to be on her side was shaken slightly when she woke next morning to a scene that was frighteningly reminiscent of the first day of her married life.

Stirring dreamily in the bed, she was stunned to find that the space beside her was empty. More than that, the sheets were cold, revealing that Vincenzo had been up and out of the room for quite some time. There was no sign of him in the bedroom, which seemed unnaturally tidy, all traces of his occupation vanished from view, and the silence in the cottage was disturbing.

Dressing hastily in the jeans and white cotton shirt she found laid out at the end of the bed, she hurried downstairs, almost stumbling in her haste, to discover the reason for the silence explained by the fact that Vincenzo was outside, dark and sombre in black jeans and a black polo shirt. But the fact that brought a cry of shock to her throat was the realisation that he had opened the car and was loading his bag—and hers—into it.

'Cenzo?' she managed uncertainly. 'What's happening? What are you doing?'

'Packing.'

It was succinct to the point of rudeness and instead of the warmth, the welcome she expected to see in his eyes, the smile she had dreamed of all night, her anxious gaze rebounded off sheer black ice, deep-frozen, set against her.

'But why?'

This was all going wrong. She had thought she would wake in his arms, or, failing that, that she would go straight into his embrace in the first moment of seeing him again.

That she would enjoy all over again the deep, drugging kisses that had tugged at her soul on the previous night, the loving greeting turning inevitably to burning passion, until they ended up in bed once more. But one glance at Vincenzo's cold, shuttered face told her only too plainly that passion was the last thing on his mind.

'What's happening? Where are—'

'We're going back.' Vincenzo didn't even let her finish the sentence. 'I've packed your things. All you have to do is to get in the car.'

'But why?' It was a cry of pain. 'I don't understand.'

'I have things I have to do.' He was clearly struggling to rein in the temper that was just on the edge of breaking. 'And I have neither the time nor the inclination to explain. Now, are you coming or not?'

The way he got into the driving seat of the car and began revving the engine left her in little doubt that if she hesitated any longer, he was perfectly capable of driving off and leaving without her. As it was, he waited only long enough for her to lock the cottage door and dash back into the car before he put it into gear, heading away down the drive while she was still fastening her seatbelt.

It took Amy some time to gather her thoughts, try to adjust to the abrupt transition from the slow, sensual awakening she had anticipated to this crazy, incomprehensible situation where the man she loved had never seemed more like a stranger to her. Just what had happened in the few short hours between falling asleep in Vincenzo's arms last night and waking up to find he couldn't get away from the cottage quick enough?

Away from the cottage and away from her? The fear that that might be the case was so intense that it clawed at her soul, driving her to turn in her seat and study Vincenzo's dark, rigid profile where it was etched against the window.

'Are you going to explain any of this?' she demanded,

putting as much force as she could into her tone to hide the panic inside.

No, aggression was quite the wrong approach. He simply ignored her all the more; concentrating on driving with an intensity that was quite unnecessary in the still, warm aftermath of the ferocious storm.

'Cenzo, please... Can you tell me what's going on?'

She reached out a hesitant hand to touch him, only to have the gentle touch repulsed by a violent movement of his arm.

'I told you. We're going back. The holiday's over; it's as simple as that. It should never have happened. None of this should ever have happened.'

'None? But I thought...'

'You thought what?' Vincenzo snapped, negotiating a difficult bend with controlled skill.

'That we—we *made love* together!'

His harsh bark of laughter froze her blood in her veins, making her shiver in distress.

'I told you before, *carissima*, you don't need love for that. All you need are two willing partners and you *were* willing—oh, so willing!'

'I...' Amy began but then sheer horror seemed to fasten round her throat like a brutal hand, choking off the words unspoken. From a dark, shadowed corner of her mind Vincenzo's words, spoken in the heat of passion the night before, came back to haunt her.

'This is how it should have been that night in Venice... This is what you owe me, *moglie mia*, what should have been mine all along...'

Oh, dear God, no! Had she truly been so completely deceived yet again? Had she let her love for him show, only to have him use it against her so cruelly, taking his revenge for the frustration of that night in Venice?

Sex and possession. Those were the words she had always associated with Vincenzo, and yet it seemed that she had needed to have her face rubbed right in it before she fully accepted just how powerful a driving force they were. He believed she was his, that she belonged to him completely, and as such he could do with her as he pleased.

'Nothing to say, *bella mia*?' Vincenzo enquired cynically. 'No comeback at all? That's not like you.'

'What is there to say when you've obviously got it all thought out and finalised in your mind?' Amy flung at him. And then, because she knew her grip on her own control was weakening and because she was determined to salvage some small degree of pride from this appalling situation, she subsided into determined silence, not saying a single word until the car pulled up outside her flat.

'Now what?' she began, only to find that she was speaking to empty air. Vincenzo had leapt from the car, opening the door and hurrying inside without even sparing her a single glance.

Did he really want to get away from her so very much? The cold that had chilled her blood seemed to have reached her heart, encasing it in a block of ice until she felt numb, dead, unable to think.

Drearily she got out of the car and followed Vincenzo into the house. He was already in his room upstairs, pulling open drawers and gathering up the contents, dumping them in a case that lay open on the bed.

'I'm going back to Venice,' he declared without preamble as soon as he saw her appear in the doorway. 'My business here is finished—except for one thing.'

'And that is?'

She no longer cared if the quaver in her voice gave her away. *Business*, was that all it had been to him? All she had been to him?

'Those papers you wanted signing. The *divorce papers*,' he added with savage emphasis when she could only stare in blank incomprehension, her brain too bruised and numbed to think. 'Get them and I'll deal with it now.'

'The *divorce papers*? But you said... Oh...'

Dazedly she shook her head, trying to bring her emotions back under control.

'Oh, I see it now!' she flung at him in a voice from which pure agony had drained all the emotion, leaving it dull and flat and lifeless. 'You got what you want from me and now you're off. You can't wait to get away—be rid of me. You—'

The ring of the bell downstairs broke into her speech, cutting her off. Left to herself, Amy would have ignored it, but to her surprise Vincenzo responded at once, moving past her swiftly and hurrying down the stairs to wrench the front door open.

'Well, Ravenelli, I'm here. So now are you going to tell me what all this is about?'

David. The last person on earth she wanted to see, particularly now.

But he was already inside the hall, and had caught sight of her hovering uncertainly at the top of the stairs.

'Amy, have you any idea what all this is about?'

'I rang David and asked him to come.' Vincenzo was cool and businesslike, totally without emotion. 'I thought you might need someone to be with you when I'd gone.'

Need someone? Couldn't he see that the only person she needed was him? That without him her life would be empty, dead?

But there was something about the way the Vincenzo spoke that caught her on the raw, pulling her up sharply. If all he wanted was to be rid of her, why would he be so concerned that she should not be left alone? And of course he had no idea how things really were between her and David or he would never have called the other man like this.

'You're leaving?' It was David who asked. 'But I thought you were both supposed to be in the Lake District until tomorrow.'

'We cut it short.'

'David, about the trip...'

Amy and Vincenzo's voices clashed, sounding as one so that David frowned his confusion. But Amy was determined to continue. A suspicion had planted itself in her thoughts and she wanted to test it out.

'There's something I have to tell you—'

'What Amy's trying to say,' Vincenzo broke in with a cool determination that silenced her simply by sheer ruthlessness, 'is that we came back early because we were having such a terrible time. It was cold, wet, boring...'

'Boring?' It was wrenched from her by shock so great that she didn't care what she said. 'Boring? Vincenzo surely you're not gong to describe some of the greatest lovemaking I've ever had in my life as *boring*?'

She had David's full attention now, all right. He was goggling at her, his eyes wide and stunned. But Amy's gaze was directed straight at Vincenzo, seeing the sudden flare of something in the darkness of his eyes. Something brief and raw that flashed on and off for a second and then was gone, covered once more by his normal self-control.

'Is this true?' David could hardly get the words out.

'Amy, don't tease!'

Vincenzo's amused reproof sounded so genuine that just for a moment Amy almost believed it, blinking hard in amazement and actually taking a step backwards in dazed reaction.

'No, of course it isn't true, David. Amy's just winding you up. As I said, we cut the holiday short because...'

But Amy couldn't focus on the rest of the explanation he was giving David. All she could think about was the first few sentences she had heard.

No, of course it isn't true. For the first time ever, certainly in all the time she had known him, Vincenzo had told a lie. Vincenzo, who swore that he would always speak the truth, had come out with a falsehood so blatant, so calculated that it rocked her sense of reality. He wasn't a man who stretched the truth as a matter of habit, so his reasons for doing so had to be something special.

But what were they?

'Look, I don't know just what's going on here,' David was definitely uneasy now. 'But don't involve me. You've got it all wrong, mate, if you think that I've got any sort of claim on Amy. There was never anything between us.'

Even as David was still speaking, Amy saw the effect his words had on Vincenzo. She saw his proud head go back as if he'd been slapped in the face, the way his dark eyes swung round to her pale face. But she didn't dare look at him, didn't dare meet that probing, searching gaze.

'I might have thought I had a chance once, but she made it plain that wasn't what she wanted. She told me that last week, before you set out for the Lake District.'

He didn't sound at all cut up about it. But then he hadn't been too bothered when she had nerved herself to break the news to him, Amy reflected. If she had needed any indication of the lukewarm quality of his feelings for her, that had been it.

'Naturally, I thought it was because of you, Vincenzo.'

'No!'

'Yes, it was...'

Once again their voice chimed together, Vincenzo's stark negative dying away before Amy's words of agreement so that 'it was' seemed to hang in the air for several nerve-stretching seconds.

'Amy,' David turned to her curiously. 'Just what is this man to you?'

'Amy...' Vincenzo began warningly, but she was determined not to listen.

Two lies in as many minutes. The only possible reason she could see for Vincenzo having used them was from some misguided belief that by doing so he was protecting her. And if he wanted to protect her, then surely that meant...

She knew what she wanted, longed for it to mean. But she didn't dare let that hope even slide into her mind. Not yet. Not until she was more sure of her ground.

'He's my husband,' she declared proudly and heard Vincenzo's muttered curse in furious Italian.

'Husband?' David had clearly decided he was out of his depth here. 'No, don't try and explain...I think it's time I took myself off and left you two to sort it out.'

With every appearance of being relieved to escape, he almost fled out the door. Amy barely saw him go; her attention was focused on Vincenzo, seeing with trepidation the dark frown her turned in her direction.

'Why the hell did you do that?' he demanded furiously.

'What?' Amy was determined to brazen it out, not to let that scowl disconcert her. 'Tell him that you were my husband? Why not? It's the truth, after all.'

'But not a truth that we want people to know about. I told you—where are those damn divorce papers?'

'You don't want—'

'Don't tell me what I want or don't want, Amy! You might be very badly shocked at just how wrong you can be. *The papers!*' he insisted vehemently when she still hesitated.

Jumping like a scalded cat, Amy moved hastily to the dresser where she kept the documents. He couldn't mean it, she told herself. Please let him not mean it.

He was fighting not to show what he felt, she was sure of that. He would take it as far as he could, right down to the wire if necessary, and then...

Hands shaking, she held out the papers to Vincenzo, then watched in horror as he snatched them from her and scrawled his name swiftly in the appropriate places.

'There.' He pushed them back at her, heedless of the way they crumpled in her hand. 'You're free. Happy now?'

How could she answer that? In the seconds that she had watched him sign his name it felt as if something had died deep inside her, something weak and fragile and very, very vulnerable had had the life crushed out of it by this final gesture.

And yet... And yet... In spite of herself, that tiny flame just would not die. She couldn't force herself to accept that this was truly it. That this was the end of her ill-fated marriage.

Vincenzo was heading for the door but he suddenly paused, swung back again.

'I'll give you your divorce, Amy, but only if you promise me one thing. You have to give me your word that you will never, *ever* think of marrying anyone like David Brooke again.'

'Didn't you hear what David said? We were never engaged—never even went out together! It was all pure fiction—not a word of the truth!'

She had thought to reassure him. Instead, it seemed that she had somehow reinforced whatever terrible thoughts were in his mind.

'Was it so bad, Amy?' he asked unevenly, his voice raw and husky.

'Was what so bad?'

'Our marriage? Was it so hateful to you that you would sooner lie and claim a relationship you didn't have in order to—'

She couldn't let him finish.

'No! It was precisely because it wasn't like that that I had to do it! When I came to you in Venice, I told myself that I wanted a divorce, that it was the only thing that was important to me. But right from the start I very nearly gave up on the idea. You only had to touch me and I was lost— I invented the idea of another man as much to protect me from myself as to shield me from you. You were right all along, you see.'

'Right?' Vincenzo's tone was flat, lifeless. His eyes looked like dark bruises above his strong cheekbones.

'About David. Vincenzo, why do you want me to promise…?'

He was moving away from her again and she had to follow him up the stairs and into his bedroom before she could ask the question once more.

'Vincenzo, I said why…?'

When he whirled round to face her, his expression made her heart clench on a wave of distress.

'Because he and his type would never make you happy. You shouldn't be with someone like that. You should be…'

'I should be…?' Amy prompted gently when he let the sentence trail off. 'With someone like you? Is that what you were going to say, Cenzo? Is it?'

The answer was in his eyes, in the pain he couldn't quite disguise, in the struggle he had to try and speak. Because she knew that no matter who else he could lie to, he couldn't lie to her.

'Is it?'

'*Si!* Yes, damn you! Yes!'

She couldn't let him go now. No matter how difficult it was, she had to push him, make him tell the truth.

'If that's the case, then why sign the papers? Why give me a divorce?'

Her heart melted as she watched him fight against the truth, and she knew the moment that he lost the battle.

'Because I can't make you happy, either. And I do so want you to be happy. But I messed up every inch of the way and it's too late now to put it right.'

'Are you sure?'

'Of course I'm damn well sure! If I hadn't known it before, I knew it last night when you wept in my arms after our lovemaking—*wept!*'

He repeated the word like a curse, emphasising his feelings with a violent gesture of one hand.

'Do you know how that made me feel? To know that I had driven the woman I love to such desperation that she cried…'

'Cenzo, no!'

She couldn't let him go on. Didn't he know what he had said? Had those wonderful, precious words, 'the woman I love' slipped out so instinctively that he wasn't even aware of having spoken them?

'It wasn't like that, truly it wasn't! I was overwhelmed with joy—with the delight of it all! My tears were tears of joy. And when I said I could never marry anyone after that—what I meant was that I could never marry anyone but you!'

Vincenzo's face was white, his eyes huge dark pools over the carved cheekbones. She'd made him listen, but she hadn't managed to convince him yet. There was only one thing for it.

She drew in a deep, calming breath, nerving herself to take the biggest chance of all, take the risk of saying the words that one of them *had* to say if they were ever to redeem this appalling situation. But even as she did so, Vincenzo was turning away again, turning back to the suitcase he had been packing.

'Oh, Cenzo, *no*!'

But then she realised that he wasn't putting anything in, he was taking something out. A small, tissue-wrapped package that he held out to her in a hand that wasn't quite steady.

'What's this?'

She couldn't look at it as he dropped it into her palm, couldn't drag her gaze away from the burning darkness of his, the white marks etched around his nose and mouth revealing the inner strain he had fought not to show.

'Open it.'

Her hands shook so badly that the package ripped, spilling open. Pouring out of the ragged hole, sparkling in the afternoon sunlight, the brilliant jewels tumbled down and onto the dressing-table beside her.

'What?' With nerveless fingers, she touched the beautiful diamonds, but couldn't bring herself to pick one up. 'Cenzo?'

He was there beside her and in his hand was the chain he had given her on their wedding day. Setting it down in the middle of glittering stones, he took both her hands in his and looked deep into her shadowed eyes.

'I promised you a diamond for each year of our marriage. These are the four I owe you—and another fifty for all the years I dreamed of being with you in the future. I want you to take them...'

'No!' Violently she shook her head, needing to stop him there. 'I can't take them, not without the marriage that goes with them.'

'You want...'

This time he didn't attempt to try and hide his feelings but let them show openly in his face. Amy saw confusion, hope, doubt, uncertainty chase one another across his stunning features. But it was hope that returned, and held, lifting her own spirits just to see it.

'Why don't you tell me about that bet?' she said softly and saw him close his eyes just once in rejection of the past.

Still with his hands in hers, he led her gently to the bed and drew her down beside him on it.

'I told you it was never meant to involve you, not specifically. And when I met you, I rejected the whole idea out of hand. I knew you were something very special right from the start, but it was all happening too quickly, and I wasn't sure of your feelings. I wanted to take things slowly.'

The hand that held hers tightened convulsively, and Amy gently stroked the cramped fingers until they eased slightly.

'I tried to break off the bet with Sal—told him he could

keep the ruby, I didn't want it. But he took that as meaning I wasn't interested in you and said he'd make a play for you himself. I've seen how my cousin works, Amy! He doesn't take no for an answer. And you were so young, I didn't think you could handle him.'

'You could have been right,' Amy admitted. 'I'd told him I wasn't interested, but he kept pestering me. So are you telling me you married me for my own protection?'

'No, for mine! When I saw Sal flirting with you, I was insanely jealous. I knew that if he hurt you I wouldn't be answerable for my reactions—and that told me how I felt about you. I couldn't let you go, not even to go back to England, not even for a second. And that was why I asked you to marry me.'

'And then Sal turned up like the serpent in the Garden of Eden?'

Vincenzo nodded his dark head slowly, his eyes fixed on her face.

'You asked if it was true that I had had a bet with Sal.'

'And you, with your obstinate insistence on always telling the absolute truth had said yes, even though it now no longer strictly applied. And I didn't give you a chance to explain. Instead, I made matters worse by my foolish declaration that I was only after you for your money. I suppose that was what was in your mind the time you came to England—when I shut the door in your face?'

'A few weeks ago you asked me which I wanted most, you or the ruby. The answer was easy—as easy as it had been four years ago—but telling you wasn't. How could I tell a woman who only wanted my wealth that she meant everything in the world to me and that I would willingly lose a thousand Ravenelli rubies if she would only come back to me?'

'But you've told me that so many times since, only I've been too blind to see. But now I know the truth, I wonder how I could ever have doubted you. Cenzo...'

Reaching up a hand to his face, she smoothed away the lines of doubt and strain, tracing the path of her fingers with her lips until her mouth met his. His response was immediate and passionate, his kiss everything she could have dreamed of. It heated her blood, set her pulse racing, woke the familiar, hungry ache deep inside. But before she could surrender to the firestorm that threatened to overwhelm them, there was one thing she had to do.

Easing herself away from Vincenzo's forceful embrace, she laid soft fingers over his mouth to silence his instinctive protest.

'I love you, *marito mio*,' she assured him softly. 'And to prove it...'

Bending down, she took the divorce papers from the floor where she had dropped them

'Why did you sign these?'

Vincenzo's sigh was deep, but he met her interrogative look without hesitation.

'The same reason as I tried to drive you away from me on our journey back from the cottage. I wanted to set you free, give you your chance to be yourself, do exactly what you wanted to do.'

'Oh, Vincenzo, don't you know that I am myself when I'm with you? That being your wife is being what I want to be? And *this* is what I think of these...'

With firm, decisive movements she ripped them in half and then in half again, repeating the action until the documents were just shreds of confetti littered over the carpet at their feet.

'There!' She surveyed the destruction with intense satisfaction. 'That's the end of that! And the real beginning of our marriage—a proper marriage this time, one built on the strongest possible foundation of love.'

The glow in Vincenzo's eyes told its own story, and his voice was husky with emotion as he said, 'I can't wait to make our private marriage a very public one. I want to tell the world that you're my wife and that I love you more than life itself.'

'I'd like that too, but right now I can think of something I'd like more…'

A mischievous smile curled Amy's lips as her wandering hands told their own story, caressing his face, tracing the outline of his lips, moving lower, lower, until a groan of response that he couldn't hold back betrayed the effect she was having on him.

'Amy…'

'Seeing as we find ourselves in a bedroom, and as we are actually man and wife, it seems a pity to waste the opportunity… Couldn't we forget about making our marriage public for just a little while? I'm sure the world can wait so we can have our own *very private* celebration.'

Her pulse rate quickened as he took her lips, his kiss promising a lifetime of happiness, a future that was so much brighter because they were together. And when Vincenzo lowered her to the bed, she went with him in a dream, but a dream from which she knew she'd never waken.

'Of course we can have a private celebration,' he whispered against her ear, his hands already busy with the buttons of her blouse, slipping them from their fastenings with a practised ease. 'I can think of nothing I want more. And for you, *innamorata*, the world will always have to wait.'

And then he bent his head and pressed his lips to her yearning body and she forgot all about the world and everything in it except for this man, her husband and her love.

*Harlequin truly does
make any time special. . . .
This year we are celebrating
weddings in style!*

**A
Walk
Down
the Aisle**
WEDDING CELEBRATION

To help us celebrate, we want you to tell us how wearing the
Harlequin wedding gown will make your wedding day special. As
the grand prize, Harlequin will offer one lucky bride the chance to
"Walk Down the Aisle" in the Harlequin wedding gown!

There's more...

For her honeymoon, she and her groom will spend five nights at the
Hyatt Regency Maui. As part of this five-night honeymoon at the
hotel renowned for its romantic attractions, the couple will enjoy a candlelit
dinner for two in Swan Court, a sunset sail on the hotel's catamaran, and
duet spa treatments.

A HYATT RESORT AND SPA   Maui • Molokai • Lanai

To enter, please write, in, 250 words or less, how wearing the Harlequin
wedding gown will make your wedding day special. The entry will be
judged based on its emotionally compelling nature, its originality and
creativity, and its sincerity. This contest is open to Canadian and U.S.
residents only and to those who are 18 years of age and older. There is no
purchase necessary to enter. Void where prohibited. See further contest
rules attached. Please send your entry to:

Walk Down the Aisle Contest

In Canada	In U.S.A.
P.O. Box 637	P.O. Box 9076
Fort Erie, Ontario	3010 Walden Ave.
L2A 5X3	Buffalo, NY 14269-9076

You can also enter by visiting www.eHarlequin.com
Win the Harlequin wedding gown and the vacation of a lifetime!
The deadline for entries is October 1, 2001.

HARLEQUIN®
Makes any time special ®

PHWDACONT1

HARLEQUIN WALK DOWN THE AISLE TO MAUI CONTEST 1197
OFFICIAL RULES
NO PURCHASE NECESSARY TO ENTER

1. To enter, follow directions published in the offer to which you are responding. Contest begins April 2, 2001, and ends on October 1, 2001. Method of entry may vary. Mailed entries must be postmarked by October 1, 2001, and received by October 8, 2001.

2. Contest entry may be, at times, presented via the Internet, but will be restricted solely to residents of certain georgraphic areas that are disclosed on the Web site. To enter via the Internet, if permissible, access the Harlequin Web site (www.eHarlequin.com) and follow the directions displayed online. Online entries must be received by 11:59 p.m. E.S.T. on October 1, 2001.

   In lieu of submitting an entry online, enter by mail by hand-printing (or typing) on an 8½" x 11" plain piece of paper, your name, address (including zip code), Contest number/name and in 250 words or fewer, why winning a Harlequin wedding dress would make your wedding day special. Mail via first-class mail to: Harlequin Walk Down the Aisle Contest 1197, (in the U.S.) P.O. Box 9076, 3010 Walden Avenue, Buffalo, NY 14269-9076, (in Canada) P.O. Box 637, Fort Erie, Ontario L2A 5X3, Canada.

   Limit one entry per person, household address and e-mail address. Online and/or mailed entries received from persons residing in geographic areas in which Internet entry is not permissible will be disqualified.

3. Contests will be judged by a panel of members of the Harlequin editorial, marketing and public relations staff based on the following criteria:

   • Originality and Creativity—50%
   • Emotionally Compelling—25%
   • Sincerity—25%

   In the event of a tie, duplicate prizes will be awarded. Decisions of the judges are final.

4. All entries become the property of Torstar Corp. and will not be returned. No responsibility is assumed for lost, late, illegible, incomplete, inaccurate, nondelivered or misdirected mail or misdirected e-mail, for technical, hardware or software failures of any kind, lost or unavailable network connections, or failed, incomplete, garbled or delayed computer transmission or any human error which may occur in the receipt or processing of the entries in this Contest.

5. Contest open only to residents of the U.S. (except Puerto Rico) and Canada, who are 18 years of age or older, and is void wherever prohibited by law; all applicable laws and regulations apply. Any litigation within the Provice of Quebec respecting the conduct or organization of a publicity contest may be submitted to the Régie des alcools, des courses et des jeux for a ruling. Any litigation respecting the awarding of a prize may be submitted to the Régie des alcools, des courses et des jeux onl for the purpose of helping the parties reach a settlement. Employees and immediate family members of Torstar Corp. and D. L. Blair, Inc., their affiliates, subsidiaries and all other agencies, entities and persons connected with the use, marketing or conduct of this Contest are not eligible to enter. Taxes on prizes are the sole responsibility of winners. Acceptance of any prize offered constitutes permission to use winner's name, photograph or other likeness for the purposes of advertising, trade and promotion on behalf of Torstar Corp., its affiliates and subsidiaries without further compensation to the winner, unless prohibited by law.

6. Winners will be determined no later than November 15, 2001, and will be notified by mail. Winners will be required to sign and return an Affidavit of Eligibility form within 15 days after winner notification. Noncompliance within that time period may result in disqualification and an alternative winner may be selected. Winners of trip must execute a Release of Liability prior to ticketing and must possess required travel documents (e.g. passport, photo ID) where applicable. Trip must be completed by November 2002. No substitution of prize permitted by winner. Torstar Corp. and D. L. Blair, Inc., their parents, affiliates, and subsidiaries are not responsible for errors in printing or electronic presentation of Contest, entries and/or game pieces. In the event of printing or other errors which may result in unintended prize values or duplication of prizes, all affected game pieces or entries shall be null and void. If for any reason the Internet portion of the Contest is not capable of running as planned, including infection by computer virus, bugs, tampering, unauthorized intervention, fraud, technical failures, or any other causes beyond the control of Torstar Corp. which corrupt or affect the administration, secrecy, fairness, integrity or proper conduct of the Contest, Torstar Corp. reserves the right, at its sole discretion, to disqualify any individual who tampers with the entry process and to cancel, terminate, modify or suspend the Contest or the Internet portion thereof. In the event of a dispute regarding an online entry, the entry will be deemed submitted by the authorized holder of the e-mail account submitted at the time of entry. Authorized account holder is defined as the natural person who is assigned to an e-mail address by an Internet access provider, online service provider or other organization that is responsible for arranging e-mail address for the domain associated with the submitted e-mail address. **Purchase or acceptance of a product offer does not improve your chances of winning.**

7. Prizes: (1) Grand Prize—A Harlequin wedding dress (approximate retail value: $3,500) and a 5-night/6-day honeymoon trip to Maui, HI, including round-trip air transportation provided by Maui Visitors Bureau from Los Angeles International Airport (winner is responsible for transportation to and from Los Angeles International Airport) and a Harlequin Romance Package, including hotel accomodations (double occupancy) at the Hyatt Regency Maui Resort and Spa, dinner for (2) two at Swan Court, a sunset sail on Kiele V and a spa treatment for the winner (approximate retail value: $4,000); (5) Five runner-up prizes of a $1000 gift certificate to selected retail outlets to be determined by Sponsor (retail value $1000 ea.). Prizes consist of only those items listed as part of the prize. Limit one prize per person. All prizes are valued in U.S. currency.

8. For a list of winners (available after December 17, 2001) send a self-addressed, stamped envelope to: Harlequin Walk Down the Aisle Contest 1197 Winners, P.O. Box 4200 Blair, NE 68009-4200 or you may access the www.eHarlequin.com Web site through January 15, 2002.

Contest sponsored by Torstar Corp., P.O. Box 9042, Buffalo, NY 14269-9042, U.S.A.

PHWDACONT2

HARLEQUIN Presents

Becky (handwritten)

Passion™

Looking for stories that **sizzle**?

Wanting a read that has a little extra **spice**?

Harlequin Presents® is thrilled to bring you
romances that turn up the **heat!**

Every other month there'll be a
PRESENTS PASSION™
book by one of your favorite authors.

Don't miss
THE ARABIAN MISTRESS
by **Lynne Graham**
On-sale June 2001, Harlequin Presents® #2182

and look out for
THE HOT-BLOODED GROOM
by **Emma Darcy**
On-sale August 2001, Harlequin Presents® #2195

Pick up a **PRESENTS PASSION**™ novel—
where **seduction** is guaranteed!

Available wherever Harlequin books are sold.

HARLEQUIN®
Makes any time special ®

Visit us at www.eHarlequin.com   HPPASSB